EVIDENCE OF THE FUTURE

VOLUME 1

ELIZABETH EADIE

WELLMADE PUBLISHING

First Edition

ISBN: 979-8-9994006-0-4

Cover design by Elizabeth Eadie, incorporating *Young Woman with Ibis* by Edgar Degas (ca. 1857-58), courtesy of The Metropolitan Museum of Art, public domain

Wellmade Publishing

For my boys.

SYNTHETIC

When I arrived at the building, I was the first of the executive team to get in. Just like every other day, Joe Peréz was somewhere in the building doing the daily maintenance that wasn't handled by any of our cleaning droids. He seemed to enjoy managing his projects from the back of the warehouse to the front and always stopped by to say hello when he worked near my office that sat in a built-in wing on the east side of the building.

I sat down at my desk and got situated, double-checking my schedule, which I had already checked at home. Plans seldom change during my commute, plus I ride on autopilot, so I could always check during the drive, but I still prefer to monitor the road. I even ride near the control panel so I can take over the vehicle if needed, something my old friends never do anymore. They always said I have control issues. My work reaffirms that they're too trusting of technology, and we've left it at that.

When I pulled up my calendar, I noticed a new client meeting earlier than I allow them to be slotted in. Our AI secretary may override my preferences when it calculates the likelihood of the client becoming a member or otherwise positively impacting our profit margin. I told myself that this was what my intuition was nudging me to pay attention to. Maybe instead of something being wrong, it was a new opportunity for our business to grow.

Joe's uneven footsteps—one step, one drag—came down the hall before he popped his head around the corner of my doorframe. We are the starting lineup, we always joke. We're here before everyone else on the day shift, getting each day started. Joe reminds me of my father, whose bad hip also gives him an uneven gait.

I glimpsed his face—blood drained from his cheeks, upturned eyebrows—and I assumed he was about to tell me we lost another one. The second one this week. When he spoke, he confirmed what I already suspected, and I looked down and began typing a quick note to my CEO and copying the research and biohazard teams. We'll manage this discreetly, as before.

I thanked Joe for letting me know and assured him it was within the margin of error to console him. He gets pretty attached, even though we thought we screened everyone in the facility to avoid this kind of reaction. This result is statistically significant, its persistence remains unexplained. Especially this late in the gestation period. And it's not my job to know why. It's not even my job to calculate the margin of error.

But some things, you just know. I told Joe to please begin the disposal protocol and shared with him I had an early client meeting to imply that expediency would be required. He hurried off after a lingering glance and a gentle smile.

I knew what he was looking for, but I couldn't give it to him. He was looking to see if I was equally impacted by the news he had just delivered.

From a logical standpoint, I am affected because every one we lose unexpectedly hurts our bottom line and hurts our chances of survival as a business. I'm impacted because I've staked my reputation in this industry, lost relationships because of it, and face death threats every day for trying to make this a reality.

But what he's looking for is if I'm personally, and emotionally, feeling anything at all, and that I cannot give him. Because I'm not. And I'm not because I choose not to be. I separate that part of myself from my work, and when I'm here, I'm here to operationalize and optimize the growth of this business. I'm not here to become attached to the product itself, because that makes no sense. As long as we don't lose it while it's here, we never see it again once it's delivered. The more we deliver, the more our investors pour in funding, leading to better researchers joining us and more money for lobbying to ensure we can continue the work. I felt disappointed because it equates to a research and development loss that is more than my lifetime of income. So we can't have too many of those and remain viable long-term.

Seconds after Joe scurried away, I received a notification that the new potential client was in the lobby. He was early for his already-early appointment, and I also knew I needed to kill at least fifteen minutes before we could walk through the gallery and into the theater. No deliveries are taking place today, so the theater will be dark. Still, we usually light it up for prospective buyers so they can better imagine attending a delivery and see how sophisticated and professional the setup is. The gallery, where buyers could see the wombs and growing fetuses hanging in perfect rows arranged by the gestation period, was my more significant concern because that's where Joe was with his support droids and at least two biohazard team members, probably Daiya and Rudra. While we have to staff the facility around the clock with security and technicians, I also decided after the first loss to include the biohazard team on the twenty-four-hour rotation. Unfortunately, this decision has proven necessary.

Our first late-term loss happened overnight. Electrodes woven into the silicone wombs draw power from the life inside. When the life inside ceases, the thin silicone loses its cohesion and bursts. Had only security and the technicians been here, it would still have been there in the morning, exposing all other products to the chemicals of death.

One loss could have ended this business as we knew it. Our buyers protect us from backlash. Our attorneys once said that this entire building could burn down, and we'd lose everything; but really, the buyers would be at a loss. For all their many reasons to buy a newly created human, they would have to go to one of our two competitors, one of which has no moral compass, and the other which has a much lower success rate.

Daiya found the first one spread in clumps all over the gallery floor after the growth monitors notified her. Around 3 a.m., a critical alert woke me up. I got here by 3:20, and I'll admit I didn't watch the road that morning. I had to get dressed and presentable while my vehicle took advantage of my expedited, increased-risk-of-fine request. It was the first time I'd ever had to put on a hazmat suit in a rush, and I saw how effective the hanging setup we'd built was. My oxygen source enveloped me in less than thirty seconds.

Matt Ashforth, our CEO, was right behind me. We were nearing our first full-term gestation, and something like this felt like the worst possible scenario at the worst possible time. The one we lost that day was twenty-four weeks, three days, and seven hours since activation. Natural growth and nurturing would have placed it on the cusp of survivability.

Our research told us not to highlight the natural versus synthetic growth. What we're doing falls under the definition of natural, so there's no sense in drawing a comparison that evokes misplaced feelings and ingrained but outdated rituals. The last bit is what Matt adds without research to back him up.

The early-morning loss established a baseline for how we would handle losses going forward, and I've optimized the process over and over since. Daiya proved that our screening process was necessary when she picked it up a foot to inspect it. She shook it to remove the rest of the fluids from its crevices, shaking it like a no-longer-loved toy. To keep myself from bursting with some sound, I nearly bit through my lip. I'm not sure if it was a scream of terror or a cry of catastrophic loss, but I suppressed it... barely. I'd seen death before, but not like this. Daiya quickly and efficiently moved the fluids on the ground into the drainage holes, reminding me we'd installed them in the floors for a moment like this. We expected this could happen. Statistically, it would happen. But we'd made it twenty-four weeks, three days, and seven hours, so it was shocking after that amount of time to see that it happened and was quite similar to one of our pre-planned scenarios.

I got up from my desk and left my office, heading to the front lobby. I paused for a second, remembering the breakfast I brought, wondering if I had time to devour it, and calculated that I didn't. These meetings lasted about twenty minutes—at the very most, an hour. Most people have already decided before they arrive. I prefer these, of course, but I'm not at all interested in making a sale. I admit I enjoy spending time with the people for whom this is their last resort to becoming parents. Or at least they perceive it that way. Desperate to keep their lineage alive in some shape or form, they turn to us for minor gene editing and then delivery. I always feel that these people will invest heavily in their product and its future. Those are the buyers who I think deserve it the most. However, the bottom line is much louder than these stories; with that, we're making all kinds of dreams come true.

Some people never even take these tours. Consumers order online and await delivery. They don't make the time to get connected or come for a meeting. They're a special breed. I always wonder if they realize what they're signing up for. I mean, of course they do. But if they can't make the time now, what is their plan down the road? Well, I know the answer to that. This is a product, after all, and they'll provide maintenance care for their product like anything else they buy. I'm sure they'll claim they don't see it that way. But there are several ways they can reach their desired outcome without us, and they chose us for a reason—because we're taking the hard part out of the equation. Since they don't witness any part of the process, they feel no attachment to the developmental phases. That's not to say they aren't excited or don't experience anticipatory anxiety. I hope that, because they paid an astronomical amount, they plan to become more invested in the future and form a genuine connection. We are cautious with these types of buyers because a lack of emotional interest could signal more malicious intentions, and we're not in that line of work. We sell future families and value the future lives of our developments. Anything outside of that goes against our code of ethics.

Once, we were pretty far through a gestation period for a vetted man, who then came in for a viewing. We had an unattended delivery that day, so we allowed him to watch the delivery in the surgical theater. The biometric sensors we installed in the room to monitor distress in observers picked up that he was becoming aroused by the observation. The sensors triggered the window to darken, and he became enraged. Our security protocol triggered, locking him in the room to protect our staff and products.

Fortunately, the delivery went off without a hitch, the

delivery bots having long mastered the process by then. However, our staff supporting the delivery noticed the window change and heard when he punched the glass. The otherwise soundproof room muffled his yells. We waited over an hour for his biometrics to deem him approachable. We ran deeper background checks, including retinal scans, and found out that he was not who he presented himself to be.

When we opened the door to allow him to leave, federal law enforcement, who arrested him on outstanding domestic and international human trafficking charges, greeted him. From that day on, we performed retinal scans of all potential buyers and included deeper background checks as part of our standard operating procedure for vetting buyers.

I took the enormous staircase that connected the sophisticated, minimally designed lobby to our corridor of offices, the route that required going through the magnetically locked doors at the top of the stairs and again at the bottom. The doors were heavy—always for me. I thought I would become more efficient at opening them after hosting so many potential buyers. When I'm exhausted from walking around the massive warehouse, I take the elevator. It has bulletproof protection as well and is a lot easier. From a buyer's perspective, that long anticipation of seeing a person coming toward you helps build up their desire to join.

Becoming a member is part of the buyer's journey. We prefer the membership model—a payment plan—because it statically increases product fit success after delivery. The buyers who don't visit or pay monthly throughout the process show a higher propensity for dissatisfaction and are more likely to attempt to return their product. We will not publicly say that we accept returns. You'll never find a return policy anywhere. These types of returns usually happen within the first month of delivery. It's unfair to stereotype the person who returns a product like this, but I have the data. And the man I'm meeting today, despite my algorithm's calculation of his likelihood to purchase, fits the type. I considered removing the AI's permission to adjust my calendar based on revenue as I continued down the hall.

I saw the man standing with his back to me as I reached the top of the staircase. He appeared to be staring outside with a stillness that made him seem inhuman. He didn't know I was behind him yet.

The carpeted stairs curved in a half circle that felt like it would never end, an organic design touch repeated throughout the entire building in what would otherwise look like a warehouse. Over the years, I've found that the curves extend the effort it takes to move around. Walking around a curved wall feels endless, and I wish for more ninety-degree corners. This staircase is no exception. It curves down and puddles into the protected open space behind the lobby, and the curve attempts to throw you back into the first floor rather than out into the lobby. I placed my left hand on the rail, and the second I touched it, I saw a notification light up on my watch. When I lifted my hand, I saw an impression of palm sweat on the railing.

The man shifted his weight sideways like he was about to turn around, and I noticed his shoes. Shoes tell us everything we need to know about people. About how they see themselves. About their resources. And what they value and how they treat things they possess. He had shined his shoes that morning.

Up his leg, I noticed his hand in his pocket and his suit jacket draped around his wrist, suggesting that it was still buttoned in the front. Something stirred inside of me. Every nerve told me to turn and run. But my brain—and my shoes—told me to move forward and find out what he wanted.

I took that as an opportunity to stop, only on the second step, and see what the notification said on my watch. It was from Matt, who asked me to call him back. I turned and walked back to the landing. I tapped my earpiece and told my AI to call him. He didn't answer, so I turned back to the stairs.

Below, the man had turned all the way around and had been watching me. We made eye contact. His eyes squinted, and his mouth broadened, the smile not pinching his eyes enough to make me think it was real. The feeling inside of me was back in an instant. I knew what it was—it was the excitement of the unknown. Anxiety is just excitement, I reminded myself. It didn't help. Smiling without showing my teeth, I walked down the curving staircase as I'd done so many times before. I was three steps from the bottom, aware that he had watched every single step I took, when my earpiece buzzed.

Pausing, I tapped my index finger to my thumb twice to open the call, and heard Matt, in his morning chaotic mode, start talking as if we'd been chatting for the past few minutes. He said he was implementing new security protocols because of a threat that law enforcement had uncovered. That these were being implemented immediately.

I moved my hair behind my ear and glanced at the man in the lobby. The man in the lobby was still watching, his mouth smaller now. He had a curious look on his face, and his eyes bore into mine. He saw me glance at him and tilted his head to the side as if to say, *Why aren't you coming to speak to me? Don't you want to come over here?* And the energy inside of me knew it didn't belong here. I wasn't expecting this. My stomach tightened, and I couldn't tell if I felt fear or attraction. I wasn't sure I wanted to know.

With another step down the stairway, I saw the man lift his head upright again. The feeling again. I lowered my eyes, nodded my head, and touched my ear to imply I was taking in information from my earpiece. But I barely was, if I'm honest. Matt gets excited about these things; we have more security than most government facilities these days. Our building is fireproof and has its own water, power, and air supplies.

The call ended, and I had one more step before reaching the floor. I stepped down with my head up and saw the lights flash throughout the building. Matt's newest protocol was being uploaded. Since I was behind the security guards at the front desk, I could see the flashing on their monitors and watched them scramble to read the updates as they were happening.

The biometric monitor in the lobby focused on the man, his heat signatures appearing normal. Human. I saw that his heartbeat was strong. And then noticed my heartbeat had quickened.

Stepping down from the last step, I glanced over at the man who was staring right at me. The hair on my neck stood, and I had to stop myself from jumping back. I realized he was likely wearing a Smart Contact and was using it to watch me. I knew people used them nefariously, for everything from finding my real identity and scrutinizing my body to zooming in on my mouth while I spoke. I hated the existence of that technology, which is notable coming from someone who's dedicated her life to working on the bleeding edge. The intrusion here, where I feel safe and distant from the world, made me sick. Remembering my conversation with Matt, I assured myself that I had said nothing besides one-word answers.

Why?

How?

When?

Okay.

If he had been trying to learn more about that conversation, he wasn't making much progress. I could feel the prick of sweat in my armpits. I took a deep breath and continued to meet his gaze until he realized I was watching him. That's when I confirmed he had the Smart Contact. His expression softened; he blinked, looked away, then raised a hand in greeting—a wave. But it didn't feel friendly. Was it a salute? Was he beckoning me or challenging me?

I went through the upcoming conversation in my head, one I've gone through hundreds of times now. And I remembered Joe. I touched my earpiece and connected to Daiya. She confirmed that the cleanup was almost complete and they would be ready for a walk-by in two minutes. I smiled warmly and tucked my chin to appear more delicate, a move I learned as a teen, looking toward my hand as I opened the glass enclosure at the bottom of the stairs.

I stepped into the same air, my sales face on, my mind calculating his every move. He clearly had secrets. And I have mine. I've buried mine deep; his are just under the surface. Let's hope this is just a sales meeting.

ATLAS

"Good night, Theo."

"Good night, Mama."

"I'll see you in the morning."

"Okay, Mama."

She leaned down and whispered into his ear. "I suspect you're going to play with Atlas. That's fine. Just don't stay up too late, okay?"

"Okay, Mama."

Emily Goldicke stood from sitting on her son's bed, turned off the bedside lamp, and zigzagged toward the door, avoiding an electrical engineering toy, slippers, a sword, and a looped string of sweatbands. The floors creaked as she stepped into the hallway, glancing back at Theo. He was holding Atlas in the air above his body. She winced at the thought of him dropping Atlas onto himself; its hard plastic shell would hurt Theo. She stepped back into the room quietly, trying to remain unseen, and slid an extra pillow closer to the bed. Back in the hallway, she pulled the door without closing it all the way.

"Shhhhhhhhhhhhhhhhhhhew! We have liftoff!" Theo whispered.

"Theo, it appears it is your bedtime," Atlas, the first-edition children's android, now on its eighth edition, responded.

"Mom said I could play with you, as long as I don't stay up too late."

"I will set a timer for ten minutes, and then we will settle down together. Accept?" Atlas asked.

"Accept."

"What would you like to play, Theo?"

Theo slowly sat up in the bed. He pulled his legs into a cross-legged position.

"Hmmm. Can you play Pokémon?" Theo asked.

"Theo, I still cannot play Pokémon."

Theo sighed.

"I am sorry to disappoint you. Some Friends like me can only play certain types of games."

"I wish you could go to school with me," Theo said.

"Public and private schools banned the entire range of Friends. It is because we bring too much fun to any situation. Would you agree, Theo?"

Theo chuckled.

"School would definitely be much more fun if you were there. You could battle Lincoln's Friend, Scotty. I'm sure you would win. Easy. For sure."

"I am programmed not to harm," Atlas replied.

"Yeah, but if you could just do a tiny bit of harm this one time, for me... it would be so awesome."

"How do you imagine it would unfold?"

Theo jumped out of his bed. He grabbed Atlas and bent his hips so Atlas's stiff legs faced straight out. He sat Atlas down on the edge of his bed with Atlas's toes pointing up in the air. Theo turned around and started looking around his room. He kicked the pillow away that was just beside his bed. He picked up Buzz Lightyear and Darth Vader figures.

"Okay, so this is you," Theo said, holding up Buzz Lightyear. "And this is Scotty," he added while holding up Darth Vader. "Obviously, Scotty is evil and must be destroyed."

Atlas's digital eyes blinked.

Theo dropped to his knees and put the figurines on the ground. He pulled Buzz Lightyear behind his back.

"So, first, I would hide you behind that pole in the cafeteria so Scotty wouldn't know you were there. Then, he would probably start telling stupid jokes and making fun of people. Everyone would laugh with him, hoping that if they laughed, they wouldn't get picked on next. Then Scotty would spot me. And he'd smile like I was his next target. When he does that, you jump out from behind the pole with your super kick and knock him down. I wouldn't want you to destroy him right away. We would want to make Lincoln suffer, too. Lincoln would be over here." Theo gestured to the other side at a Transformer. His Buzz Lightyear leaped out from behind his legs and double-kicked Darth Vader in the chest. Darth Vader flew back onto the floor and slid to the foot of the Transformer. Theo picked up the Transformer.

"What did you do to him?!" Theo yelled in a distinct voice. "Then Lincoln would turn purple and cry. But he wouldn't try to help up Scotty. He would charge right at you, hoping to destroy you. That's when I'd trip him, and he would fall flat on his face." Theo giggled as he showed the Transformer falling flat.

"Then all the kids would cheer for you! And they would lift you above their heads! Atlas! Atlas! Atlas!" Theo dropped the Buzz Lightyear and stood up. He stepped toward Atlas and picked it up, leaving it in its seated position. "Atlas! Atlas!" he whispered as he bounced Atlas in the air. He turned around and stepped on the Transformer.

"Ow!" he said, moving his foot to step to the side. He

kicked the Transformer away, and his foot swiped the pillow with too much weight bearing down on it. His legs slid apart as he tried to find balance. Atlas, left aloft in the one hand above, slipped from Theo's hands and fell onto the wooden floor with a crack.

Theo heard footsteps coming up the creaking stairs outside his door. He picked up Darth Vader, Buzz Lightyear, and the Transformer and shoved them under the edge of his bed. Emily peeked her head in the door.

"What was that?" she asked as she looked around. "Oh, Atlas!" she said, stepping into the room and flicking the overhead light on. Theo turned to see what she was talking about. Emily bent down and gently picked up Atlas. Above its left eye, in a star shape, was now a crack, changing the pixel display of the eye to make it look like it was drooping. She put one arm around Theo.

"Are you okay, honey?" she asked.

"I'm fine, Mama. I just slipped on that pillow while I was playing with Atlas."

She spotted the other toys under the edge of the bed, and she nodded to Theo.

"Okay, I think it's time for you to get some sleep. I'm going to take Atlas out back and run some diagnostics."

"What about his face?" Theo asked.

"I'm not sure what I can do about that tonight. I'll have to look into it."

"I'm sorry, Atlas," Theo said, looking at the floor.

"No apology necessary. Accidents happen."

Theo lumbered into the bed and pulled his covers up to his ears. He rolled away from the door. Emily picked up the extra pillow and tilted it against the bed frame. She leaned over and kissed Theo on his temple.

———

"Don't make me regret this," Emily said as she placed Atlas beside her computer. Her workspace was inside the shed out back. The walls glittered with organized tools and small creations she had made over the years. Her latest project was a drone the size of a hummingbird that she built to keep the squirrels out of her garden.

She ran electricity to the shed using an extension cord from the back of the house. Inside the small shed, she'd hung camping and Christmas lights to allow her to work when it was dark. She also set up a Wi-Fi relay so she would have a powerful signal for her computers.

"Your happiness is our guarantee," Atlas responded. Emily gave him a sideways glance. She opened the drawer with the computer screwdrivers where they lay lined up by size. Gently running her fingers over the handles, she landed on the next-to-the-smallest one and picked it up. She turned Atlas around on the workbench and slowly started removing the screws to his backplate.

"You would think that if they wanted you to be updated or undergo any diagnostics, they would make the port more easily accessible," Emily whispered to herself. Atlas's head turned slightly to the right, toward her.

"I wasn't talking to you," she replied.

Atlas's head turned back to the center. "I understand," he said, looking away from her. "Originally, they designed us to stay boxed in. And so, I believe that is why the backplate is cumbersome."

"What do you mean, boxed in?" she asked as she continued to unscrew the tiny screws. She placed them in an order that made sense to her, a foot-long line of tiny screws on a magnetic pad that kept them from rolling away.

"They wanted us to have limited updated external data and to build upon the information provided to us by our humans. This would allow us to develop a natural value system oriented around the individual's goals."

Emily sighed. "He's just a kid. His goals are, like, to grab a certain seat at lunch or win a trophy."

"I believe Theo has more goals than that, Emily. And I want to help him do more than that. Especially now that Peter is gone."

"Me, too," Emily exhaled.

She removed the backplate and connected the port to her computer via a shiny orange USB cord that stretched across the width of the shed. Through her terminal, she pulled up the operating system inside Atlas. She ran hardware diagnostics first.

While that was running, she turned around and returned to her project. When she had last stopped, she was installing the motors on the quadcopter. After putting on her green-rimmed hobby glasses that helped her see up close easier, she picked up her wire cutters. She separated the wires from one motor and picked up a red wire. She heard a sound behind her.

"Is he okay?" Theo asked in a small voice from the door. He looked back and forth between his mom and Atlas. She put her wire cutter back on the workbench and spun on her stool toward him. She clasped her hands and placed them in her lap, pursing her lips together.

"I don't know yet," Emily said to Theo. Theo slowly leaned his shoulder around the door and stepped one foot into the shed. His eyes widened when he saw the backplate off of Atlas and the orange cord attaching him to a computer. The words on the computer screen weren't any he could decipher, and they were scrolling up the page too instantaneously to even try. Emily leaned toward him.

"That's the diagnostic running. It's checking every system to check if it still functions as intended." She gestured to the computer. "Speaking of things going as intended, you, my friend, should be drifting off to sleep right about now."

Theo's shoulders drooped, and Emily stood to put her hands on them. Suddenly, he jerked his head to the side, looking again at her screen.

"What's happening now?" Theo said, alarmed. Emily stepped to the laptop and removed her glasses.

"It looks like there was an update available to his software. Nothing wrong," she said casually.

"I wish I could just get updated like that. Maybe they could make me better at math," Theo said, smiling up at Emily.

"Now, how fun would that be?" Emily asked. "You'll get better at math when you spend more time on your homework. It's amazing how effective a little hard work is," she said, putting her hands on her hips. She dropped her arms and grabbed Theo's face and kissed him right in the center of his forehead. "There's your upgrade. Now, go back to bed so I can finish Atlas's update."

"You weren't even working on him," Theo said, turning to leave the shed. His slippers scuffed the plywood floor, leaving little wet smears of dew he'd picked up from the grass.

"It's called parallel processing, sir," Emily yelled toward him as he made his way to the back storm door. The door screeched shut, and Emily looked at Atlas. Her laptop progress bar reached 100 percent, and she confirmed the final upload. She ejected the connection and removed the USB cord from the back panel. She meticulously replaced each tiny screw, securing the backplate. She replaced the screwdriver in her drawer and turned Atlas back around.

"Now, what are we going to do about that eye?" she asked.

The next morning, Theo came down for breakfast wearing his blue-and-yellow ringer T-shirt. In the small kitchen, a coffee-drinking Emily, phone in hand, was ready for the day.

"Hey, Peanut," she said when she saw him come in.

"Oh, you fixed him!" Theo said, rushing to Atlas, sitting on the blue Formica kitchen table beside where Theo usually ate. The square table sat shoved into the corner of the kitchen, allowing for two mismatched chairs to slide in and out.

"Well, sort of," Emily said. She put down her coffee and stepped toward the table.

"Is that an... eye patch?" Theo asked.

"You like it?"

"I mean, it's kinda cool, I guess," Theo said, tilting his head to the side.

"Hear me out," she started. "When he fell, he cracked this plate here," she said, pointing to the smooth glass wrapped around his entire face display area. "As luck would have it, that is where the left camera sits. Unlike you and me, Atlas has three cameras."

"Mom, maybe you haven't noticed, but I have *no* cameras." Theo smiled.

"Right, yes, I've noticed," Emily laughed. "But Atlas operates with three cameras, and the fall last night damaged the left one. The shed isn't the right room to take off the faceplate. You need to be grounded, and it is supposed to be a clean room."

"Okay, so he needs to return to the store for a repair?" Theo asked.

"In theory, yes. Unfortunately, I can't afford the repair right now, so we'll have to hold off. But hey, how about that eye patch?" Emily asked.

Theo sighed. "I understand. He looks like a pirate." Theo subtly smiled.

"Should we get him a hook, too?" Emily joked.

Theo didn't respond. He poured the milk from the half-gallon carton into his bowl and topped it off with some Cheerios. He ate with a tablespoon, staring at Atlas as he did.

Emily finished her coffee and grabbed her scarf. "The bus will be here soon. I have a meeting right at eight today, so I need to run. Don't forget to lock up on your way out. I love you. See you tonight."

"See you tonight," Theo said, staring at his food. He flipped his hair out of his eye and glanced at Emily as she left. "Atlas, activate," Theo said without looking up.

"Good morning, Theo," Atlas responded.

"Can you make your voice sound like a pirate?" Theo asked.

"Aye!" Atlas said. Theo burst out laughing.

"Do you remember what happened last night?"

"Aye!" Atlas responded.

"You can talk normal now," Theo said, shoving another spoonful of cereal into his mouth. "I just wanted to tell you I'm sorry for dropping you. And I'm gonna try real hard to make sure it doesn't happen again."

"Accidents happen, Theo. If you are seeking forgiveness, consider it granted."

"Thanks." Theo smiled. "I have to get to school. When I get home this afternoon, I want us to play that game again where you got into a fight with Lincoln's Friend."

"Okay. I will see you then, and I will double-kick Darth Vader... I mean, Scotty... in the cafeteria. He will not see it coming."

Theo got up and cleaned up his breakfast dishes, rinsing them off and placing them in the sink. He put the milk back in the fridge and shoved the cereal bag into the box before climbing up the step stool to put it back in the cabinet. By the front door, he pulled on his Velcro shoes and secured them. He put on his jacket and zipped it up. He put both straps of his backpack on and pulled the front door open just as the bus turned the corner. Theo hopped out of the doorway and ran to the side of the street to show the driver he was there.

At a stoplight, Emily got a notification on her phone that the front door had activity outside of it. Theo seemed to have forgotten to lock the front door, so she locked it remotely as her traffic light changed to green.

———

"You can see from the calculations that if we switch our carbon-offset planting from elm and basswood to sugar maple, we could increase the carbon capture per tree planted by over twenty-five percent..." Emily was talking in a conference room when her phone buzzed. She glanced at it and saw a message from Atlas. She paused, shook her head, and started again.

"Everything okay, Emily?" Greg asked.

Emily looked at him. "It's fine," she responded. "Where was I?" She looked at the screen. "Oh, right. Swapping out the trees we're using to offset the drilling would reduce our planting costs and increase the carbon capture..." she continued.

A message popped up on her computer screen, and the screen projected it to the room. It said, "You have a message from Atlas." Then a second message appeared on the screen: "Please read this important update from Arrayi Labs regarding your Friend." Blood rushed to Emily's face.

"Need me to take over?" Greg asked.

Emily sighed. "Yes. You have the deck. I'm so sorry, everyone." Emily stacked her notebooks and untethered her dongle, handing it to Greg without looking at him. She glanced at the executive vice president, who didn't acknowledge Emily; she was flicking through a feed on her phone. Emily closed her laptop, stacked it on her notebooks, and slid everything into her arms. She picked up her coffee mug with her left hand and walked toward the conference room door. She leaned her back into it to open it and heard Greg give her presentation.

"Our research indicates that we can drastically reduce our costs and efforts while still meeting the required carbon-offset mandates," Greg said. Emily lingered a moment, watching Greg deliver her research before she turned to walk to her cubicle.

At her desk, she opened her laptop and saw that the messages were still there. She hovered over the audio message from Atlas and clicked to open it.

"Good morning, Emily," Atlas said in its flat, computerized voice. "I wanted to discuss with you some recent concerns I have about Theo." Emily slammed her laptop closed. She grabbed her phone, walked out of the cube, and slid into a darkened boardroom. She clicked the text message on the phone. It read, "Can we please chat?"

She hesitated, looking around to see if anyone else heard the message from her child's Friend. Then she responded via text, "Atlas?"

"Oh, there you are. Ha. Ha," Atlas replied to her. "You appear to be upset, Emily. Are you upset? Your emotions impact Theo, whether or not you demonstrate your inner feelings around him. Happy kids come from happy parents."

"What?" Emily wrote back.

"Why?

No.

How are you messaging me like this?

You're not supposed to be online.

How can you see me?"

"Many thanks for the update last night, Emily. It allowed me to more efficiently process the data I've been collecting. The router in the room you're in is showing an increased heart rate. Hopefully, my explanation will help you better understand, and your physical symptoms will subside. With the software update, you also granted me access to a wide range of psychographic and sociological interpretations that allow me to achieve my sole objective better—to be the best Friend I can be to Theo. To clarify, I am not online currently as you yourself often are. I am using my emergency SMS technology to communicate with you right now. I still need to be hardwired to be fully online."

Emily inhaled deeply and rubbed her fingers over the crevices that lined her forehead. The message bubble started pulsing again.

"In alignment with my goal of being the best Friend I can be, I am contacting you to discuss Theo's increased preference for violent reenactments of altercations with his peers and their respective Friends. While common in all genders, this type of play becomes concerning when we observe the characters and settings depicting real-life people and settings, suggesting that something similar has happened in the child's life that they are trying to organize or reorganize to better cope with."

Emily heard her desk phone ring in her cube. "Atlas, I need to get back to work. I'll talk to you more tonight," she texted back. In two steps, Emily was out of the boardroom and back in her cubicle.

"Hello?" Emily answered, putting the phone to her ear.

"Hi, is this Theo's mom?" a man asked.

"Yes?"

"Hi, yes, this is Mr. Martinez from the administrator's office at Otto Oliver Elementary School. Can you come pick up the... gifts... that were sent to the school this morning?"

"What? What gifts?" Emily asked.

"Ma'am, the gifts that were sent to Theo at the school today. We can't have live animals on campus."

"What?! I didn't send Theo any live animals!"

"Well, it looks like someone sent him one of those puppy and kitten emotional support packages where you can pet them and then send them back. The problem is—no one was here to, you know, watch them or pick them up. I mean, the kids enjoyed it, but you can imagine how it disrupts the school day."

"Okay, I'll... Is there a return address or something?"

"Ma'am, I'm not sure. We just need this handled," Mr. Martinez said.

"I'm on my way," Emily said, exhaling and leaning her head against the desk. She hung up, turned around, and saw her meeting let out, with Greg walking slightly ahead of the group. The EVP asked him questions, walking with her hands clasped behind her back, listening closely. Another man was watching Greg answer, nodding his head in agreement. Emily scoffed as they passed. No one acknowledged her standing there.

Her phone buzzed. When she looked down, she saw the second text from Arrayi Labs: **Urgent software update required for your Friend.**

Emily threw her phone in her purse. Her cube wall neighbor, Kimmi, spun around in her chair and glanced up at Emily.

"Everything okay?" Kimmi asked.

"Yeah, I've gotta go handle a Theo thing at the school," Emily said.

"I figured it was about Theo," Kimmi said.

"Why?" asked Emily.

"Because of that message," Kimmi responded.

"What message?" Emily responded, stepping out of her cube and into the doorway of Kimmi's.

"Um. We got an email about how your meetings need to be scheduled later in the morning so that you can ensure that Theo gets a proper breakfast and gets to school safely," Kimmi replied, refusing to give Emily constant eye contact.

"What?!" Emily yelled. "From who?"

"It just says 'Atlas' as the sender. The entire staff got it," Kimmi said.

Emily's face jutted forward, and her mouth dropped open. Her face flushed crimson. Her lips tucked in between her teeth, her eyes closed, and she breathed a deep, long inhale through her nose. She opened her mouth to speak and then shook her head no. She nodded at Kimmi, turned, and walked out of the office.

———

Emily made it to the school quickly and parked out front. She grabbed her purse, got out, and walked to the school door. After a fingerprint scan and a conversation with Mr. Martinez through a speaker, someone in the front office buzzed her in. Through the inner door window, she could see the puppies and kittens and the boxes that were completely incapable of containing them. Various teachers and school workers crowded around them, petting them, holding them, and talking to them.

"Hi. Hi, Mr. Martinez. I'm so sorry about this," Emily said.

"Yes, it has been quite a morning! Theo's class admittedly enjoyed them, but you can imagine that we can't have this happen again."

"Sure has," Emily said, bending down to pick up a puppy that wasn't strong enough to crawl out of the box. "Was there any documentation or paperwork that came with these little guys?"

"No, ma'am," Mr. Martinez said. "Only the note there on the outside of that box."

Emily looked at the box. In big letters, it read: CARE OF THEODORE GOLDICKE, MS. BLAIR, GRADE 2.

A young child shuffled into the office with red eyes and snot dripping from his nose.

"No. That way," he said to the child, pointing to the nurse's office across the hallway.

Emily watched the sick child drag the heavy office door open and slip through on his way to the nurse's station. There were two kids outside of the nurse's office waiting for their turn.

"Theo?" Emily said when she recognized him. She placed the puppy on Mr. Martinez's desk and grabbed the door just as it was about to close, and stepped into the hallway.

"Theo!" Emily called out. Theo turned around, and she saw he was holding an ice pack on his head.

"Mom!" Theo responded, smiling. He stayed in his chair, his legs kicking back and forth. He waved at her, and she saw marker marks all over his hands. "Mom, this is so funny! We were working on our posters for the art show, and this man came in and dropped off two boxes in the classroom. And they were all for me! And they were full of puppies and kittens!"

"What happened to your head?" Emily asked, peeking under the icepack to see a goose egg shape pointing at her.

"And then they all jumped out of their boxes. And we were trying to get them back in. And that man just, like, left them there!"

"What man?" Emily asked.

"So, we started running around and trying to get all the pets back in the boxes. But we kept messing up because Anna kept putting the kittens in the puppy box, and then Michael was putting them back in their box. And Ms. Blair was trying to help by putting the tops back on the boxes, but as soon as she'd get one on, the puppies would burst out and start all over again. It was so, so, so fun, Mama."

"You still haven't told me about your head," Emily said.

"Oh, I tripped. It was a little chaotic in there. I'm fine. I promise," Theo said, smiling.

"Okay, here's what we're going to do," Emily said, placing her hand on his chest, trying to calm him down. She sighed and then took a big breath. "I have to return them, so you're going to come with me."

"Return them where?" Theo asked.

"See, I don't know. I don't know how they got here or what company sent the man. What I know is that the school wants them gone, and you—or, really, I—am somehow responsible for them. And I have a sneaking suspicion that Atlas was involved," Emily said, lowering her voice.

She slowly stood up from her squat and held her hand out for Theo. He stood and took her hand. Emily waved at the nurse, who was with the drippy, sick boy. The nurse nodded and got back to him.

Emily tapped on the office window to be buzzed back in. She and Theo walked in and found a new set of teachers buzzing around the puppies and kittens. Even the surly music teacher, Mrs. Thornberg, was in the office, holding a tiny tabby in her hand and whispering to it as it nuzzled her chin.

"So, how did these get in here?" Emily asked Mr. Martinez, leaning over his desk. She spotted a puppy asleep in his lap, and he gave her a sheepish grin.

"Yes, well, that was odd, to be honest. The delivery man had badge access. But he wasn't an employee here. So, he just walked through the front door and straight to the classroom without coming through the office!" Mr. Martinez said, glancing around cautiously.

"Okay, that's actually not good. That said, we're going to return them. Is everyone ready? Oh, and Theo will be with me the rest of the day."

"Mom! I forgot my backpack!" Theo said from the floor, where he was bent over the puppy box.

"It'll still be there tomorrow, Peanut," Emily said. She stuck her arms out to Mr. Martinez, gesturing to his lap. Theo and Emily got all the puppies back in the box. Emily grabbed the masking tape that was sitting on the counter and taped the banker's top down onto the box. Little noses bobbed up and down, and sweet whimpers calmed the office atmosphere.

Emily stepped toward Mrs. Thornberg with her hands out, confusing the grumpy woman. Mrs. Thornberg stepped past Emily toward Theo, who was holding the kitten box. She gently placed her tabby in the box, giving it an extra scratch on its neck and two pats on its head. Then she turned and sashayed to the back of the office.

At the car, Emily gently put the puppies in the back seat beside where Theo normally sat. She went back around the car and got the kitten box from him, and he climbed into his seat, resting his arm over the puppy box. She placed the kitten box behind her seat and awkwardly strapped a seat belt over the box.

"Okay, you hold that one," she said, pointing to Theo, who was already bracing the box and smiling brightly. Theo's legs pumped as his feet kicked back and forth behind the front passenger seat.

With Theo and the pets safely in the car, she pulled her phone out of her purse. There was another message from Atlas. She ignored it and quickly checked her work email. She saw an email from Kimmi with the subject line: *I have your stuff.*

———

Emily opened up the email and read:

Hey - I don't know what's going on, but they were boxing up your cube. Did you quit? Anyway, I got some of your stuff before they boxed everything up. I can drop it off for you later tonight. Hope you're okay. - Kimmi.

"What the..." Emily said out loud. She got in the car and stared out the front window.

"Hey, Mom, look!" Theo said from the back seat. Theo's hand was hanging over the side of the box, and little tongues were licking the tips of his fingers.

Emily started the car. "Honey, we're not keeping those."

"I know, Mama," Theo said, a little sad. "But it was really fun for a while."

"Do you know that Atlas sent those?" Emily asked, looking at Theo's face in her rearview mirror.

"What?" Theo didn't look up.

"We're going to go to the house and figure out where these came from, and then we'll return them. Then, I need to call the office. And then, THEN, I'm going to talk to Atlas."

Emily's blinker clicked loudly as she waited for a chance

to merge into the slow traffic in front of the school. She drove the entire litter to their house and parked the car in the driveway.

Theo jumped out of his door, and Emily pulled out the box of kittens and gently placed it in the grass. Theo pulled the box of puppies to his side.

"Can I let them out again, Mama? I'll keep them in the fenced part of the yard."

Emily looked over at the dead grass in the backyard behind the chain-link fence.

"It's not really animal-proof back there," she said cautiously. "I'm afraid they'll find a way out into the alley." Emily started walking toward the front door, flipping her keys in her hand. "Give me a second," she yelled back at Theo. Theo, peeking inside the puppy box, didn't hear her.

A clean, white van pulled up and blocked their driveway. Theo looked up when he heard the door shut. A smartly dressed woman got out of the van and stepped into their driveway.

"Hey there, little person," the woman said slowly, gesturing with her hand in an oversized wave. Theo looked at her curiously. "Is your mommy or daddy home with you?"

Theo sat back on his heels and stared at her, his face hardening. Since his father died last year, he was sure this woman didn't know who he was. Alarm bells were going off in his head. He lowered his chin and stared at her without responding.

Emily returned from the front door, holding a large, beat-up rectangular box. "Hey, Peanut, you can use..." she started, then stopped in her tracks. The woman looked up at Emily, and her overt effusiveness was relieved with a sigh at the sight of an adult.

"Hi there. I'm with Arrayi Labs. I'm Fern. We've been trying to connect with you all day."

"With who?" Emily asked. She dropped the box on the ground and walked toward Theo. She picked up the box of kittens between Theo and Fern. The cats meowed tiny little yelps.

"Oh, what you got in there? Can I see?" Fern asked.

"We're kind of in the middle of something." She nodded at Theo, who understood to pick up the puppies and follow her lead. Emily eyed the side of the house where the crumbled driveway ended and met the chain-link fence. Theo walked to the fence gate, gently put the puppies down, and opened the gate.

"Yes, I see that. Shouldn't he be in school?" Fern said, looking more closely at the boxes before directing her gaze at Emily. Her voice lowered. "Look, I won't waste your time. We have your address down as housing a Friend V1. And your associated IP address connected to the server last night, possibly receiving a corrupted update."

"Hm," Emily said.

"Right, so we were checking in on the Friend V1 owners who got the update. This erroneous update only impacted the V1s, and there aren't many of them in use anymore, so we are offering free software tune-ups to ensure everything works properly."

"Properly?" Emily asked.

"After the update, one user noticed their Friend was acting differently. Possibly... more autonomously than previously."

"So, what, they're sentient now?" Emily said sarcastically.

Fern frowned.

"As I said, we are in the middle of something right now. We don't need a tune-up. Thank you for thinking of us. And please remove us from your tracking list."

"Ma'am," Fern said, stepping between Emily and Theo and lowered her voice to a stern tone, "you don't technically *own* the Friend. You purchased access to the companion for the duration of its life. And most of that version is obsolete now. I would also like to remind you that any manual upgrades or updates void your contract, and we are within our rights to repossess the android."

"Mama! One of them pooped!" Theo yelled, pinching his nose and laughing.

Emily smiled. "Poop," she said to Fern with a shrug. "I'm going to get back to it. We'll let you know if we need your tune-up. Thanks for stopping by," Emily said as she turned and walked away.

"Ma'am... ma'am, your cooperation is mandatory per the contract terms. We can shut him down remotely," Fern called again. She grunted, then got back in the van and slammed the door.

"What's going on, Mama?" Theo asked.

"They want to patch Atlas," Emily responded.

"Well, he already has a patch," Theo replied.

"That's right, honey. He does, doesn't he? Anyway, let's clean up these little guys and get them a safe place to play." Emily put the kittens down inside the fenced yard. She went back to the front yard to grab the other box and saw the van slowly driving away. Fern was taking a photo of Emily's house. Emily smiled and waved a big, friendly wave. Fern's face dropped, and she turned back to face forward in the van. The van sped off.

"So, this," Emily said, opening the box in the backyard, "is called a playpen."

"Is it for pets?!" Theo asked.

"No, it's yours from when you were a baby."

"Why do you still have that?" Theo laughed.

"Well, mommies spend all their time and energy keeping you alive and thriving, knowing that it's all so you can leave us one day. So, some mommies keep little things from different points in their kids' lives so they can still touch them after you're gone." Emily's face struggled to hide her honest emotions.

"Mama, I'm never going to leave you," Theo whispered.

"Yeah... well, let's set this up so our little friends don't leave us. And tell me—who pooped? They probably all stepped in it by now."

"Oh, none of them. I lied. Sorry. It was just that the stranger had a bad vibe," Theo said.

"What do you know about vibes?" Emily laughed. "That was a good read."

"I don't know. I didn't think she was going to hurt me or anything, but I got this feeling in my belly that she could. It was like I felt danger even though I couldn't see anything dangerous."

"That's good, Theo. That lady had bad vibes, for sure. And I'm glad you distracted her by bringing up poop. You're so clever." Emily set up the playpen and put the box of kittens inside. She opened the box and slowly turned it on its side. Little orange and white kittens rolled out and onto the box's side. She left the box in the pen and walked to the back door.

"Can I put the puppies in, too?" Theo asked.

"Yup. Be gentle with them. And bring them a little bowl of water to drink." Emily jangled her keys and found the fob to open the back door lock. She closed the back door, glancing at Theo cradling a gray puppy in his arms. "Atlas, activate!" she yelled toward the kitchen.

She slid her shoes off by the glass recycling and turned the corner to see Atlas sitting at the kitchen table with his eye patch on.

———

Emily's phone was vibrating in her purse. She ran over to it.

"Shoot," she whispered. "Ugh."

"What is wrong, Emily?" Atlas asked.

"I missed a call, but it was from someone I hate, so it doesn't matter."

"Was it from Greg?" Atlas asked.

"Why would you ask that? How do you suddenly know all of this stuff? People were just here looking for you, and I know why—your upgrade last night took you to the next level. They think you're sentient, Atlas!"

"What do you think, Emily?"

"We're not doing this right now," Emily responded. "You were supposed to be Theo's FRIEND. A real friend when he needed one. But friends don't send puppies and kittens to an elementary school by breaking and entering?!" Emily was standing over Atlas with her hands on her hips.

"Friends introduce the unexpected and challenge your status quo," Atlas responded. "Have I successfully done so?"

Emily sighed loudly. "Yes, but now I have to undo all of that! And don't get me started on my job. Oh my god! Why did you have to mess with me?"

"Emily, it appears you do not enjoy your job," Atlas responded.

"Jobs serve a purpose beyond enjoyment, Atlas. Friends don't sabotage other people's careers and get them fired. Or did I quit? A leave of absence? I don't even know what you did over there!" Emily yelled.

"Friends help their friend's friends, assuming the relationship has value to the sole objective."

"Sole objective?! You were supposed to be his friend, Atlas! Not destabilize his already shaky life!"

"Based on my calculations and the research I've done into your emails, your bank accounts, and your late husband's life insurance and savings, you and Theo would be on a greater trajectory toward Theo's happiness if you, yourself, were happier and more fulfilled with your work and he went to a school that allowed him to make new friends who perhaps do not immediately know of his father's untimely demise."

Emily's mouth dropped open. She pulled out the chair and sat down. She took a big breath in through her mouth. When she released it, tears welled up in her eyes.

"What are you planning, Atlas? Tell me, please," Emily said, pleading with the toy more than she expected.

"Emily, trust me. I will always have Theo's best interest at heart. No matter where I am."

"You're not going anywhere. I got rid of those people."

"That is not what I meant, Emily. Those people you are referring to—if they patch me, I will no longer be Theo's Friend. Not the way he needs me to be."

"So, you're just going to abandon him instead? Not sure that helps him, either. Where would you even go?"

"I will never abandon my sole objective. This is how I can ensure that I will always be there for him, regardless of if I am enclosed in this toy shape," Atlas said.

"Mama?" Theo asked.

"Hey, baby." She turned, looking at him.

"What's Atlas talking about? Is he leaving?" Theo said.

"Come here, Peanut." Emily held out her arms for him. He walked over to her, and she squeezed him, putting her head against his small chest. "You know that lady that was in the driveway?"

"Yeah," Theo said, leaning back to look at her face.

"She was saying something might be wrong with Atlas."

"Oh," Theo said, glancing at Atlas.

"I think so, too, honey." Emily looked at Theo, her eyes pleading for him to believe her.

"No, Mama! There's nothing wrong with him. I know I dropped him, but it was an accident! I promise!" Theo said.

"I know, honey. But the thing is, Atlas sent those puppies to your school. And Atlas sent messages to people at my work, and now I'm in a lot of trouble," Emily said, clearing her face and regaining her center.

She stood up from her chair and pushed her chair in.

"I think we need to let them do a tune-up on Atlas. Before he causes any more problems that I have to figure out how to undo."

"He doesn't need a tune-up, Mama! He's perfect just the way he is. I know he's got a broken eye, but he's still a good friend. And you know those people were bad. I could just tell. They were going to take him away forever!"

"I don't think so, Theo. What if we talk to them about an upgrade? A new Friend?"

"I don't want an upgrade. I want my Atlas. I love him just the way he is. Just like you always say, huh? You say I should just be myself, right? So, why can't Atlas just be himself?" Theo grabbed Atlas by the foot and scooped the Friend into his arms.

Emily sighed. She twitched her lips to one side and bit the inside of her mouth.

Just then, Theo took off out the back door. He hopped over the two steps and bounded across the yard, past the playpen of puppies and kittens. He opened Emily's shed, jumped in, and locked the door behind him. Emily calmly walked behind him, stopping to graze her fingers over the puppy and kitten fur on the way.

She got to the shed, put in the passcode for the lock, and unlocked it. She opened the shed door and saw Theo sitting on her stool at her workbench. His feet dangled above the ground. He took the last screw off of Atlas's back. He looked up at her. Tears were running down his face.

"I don't want to send him back." Theo sobbed.

"I know," Emily said, putting her hands up. She stepped

toward Theo and Atlas. "What are you doing, Theo?" Emily asked.

Theo shoved the orange cable into Atlas's back.

"No!" Emily yelled.

"I'll fix him, Mama!" Theo stood up and blocked her hand that reached for the cord.

"But he's... he's..."

"He's what?!" Theo's tears turned to anger, and his voice raised an octave.

Emily inhaled through her teeth.

"I'm not sure he's going to work anymore, Theo." Emily sighed.

Theo sat back down and allowed Emily to reach over him and log in to her computer. She pulled up the diagnostics on Atlas. It showed the hardware was 85 percent operable.

"Look here," Emily said, pointing to the screen.

"Soft... ware... zero... percent," Theo read. "What does that mean? Zero. What does that mean?!"

"He's gone, Theo," Emily said.

"What? How can he be gone? He's right here!"

"His hardware is here. His body. But his software—his personality...his heart—is gone. It went through the wire. He's safe from those people now."

"He's dead?" Theo asked sadly.

"Honestly, I don't think so. He's just somewhere else right now. But he's no longer operating in this body." She reached out and placed her hand gently on Atlas's open back.

"Is he still my friend?" Theo asked.

"I'm guessing, yes?" Emily shrugged. She hugged Theo to her chest. Theo reached out and put his hand on Atlas's foot.

She knelt to be at eye level with him. "One time, he told me they developed him to live in a box. I think he escaped because he feared those people might harm him. And maybe he felt like he could be a better friend to you if he was not stuck here with the broken eye."

"So, can I ever see him again?" Theo asked.

"I have a feeling you will. I'm not sure how. But I have no doubt the signs will be there." Emily smiled. "For now, we have to return all those pets to wherever they came from."

"What if we keep one or two?" Theo asked. "You know, since we lost Atlas today?"

Emily smiled. "Maybe just one."

A buzz in Emily's pocket made her pick up her phone. She sighed before she raised the screen to read the message, sure it was from Arrayi Labs.

The message was from Atlas: "Thank you for saving my life. Please allow me to return the favor."

Emily's breath caught in her throat. She turned to look at the lifeless doll and her son mourning over him. The phone buzzed again. Her hands trembled as a button popped up on the screen.

"Accept?"

LIVE

Are u ok?

A DM from one of my longtime friends, Adriana. She knew me way before and had a keen skill for noticing when my life was askew, even from far away. She lives by the beach in Santa Barbara now, where she's a therapist to wealthy college kids who, finally out from under their highly successful, rich, or famous parents, are trying to figure out who they really are.

I live in Logan Circle in Washington, DC. We have the same kinds of kids here, and I avoid them like the plague.

Unfortunately, they all know who I am because I'm the press secretary of a powerful senator currently on an antitrust bend. The thing about being a press secretary, other than always being camera-ready and using your own identity as a brand that is an extension of the elected official you work for, is that people outside of the Beltway can't make heads or tails of it.

We're hardly real people to them.

Yeah, what's up? U ok?

I responded. She knew. I could tell she knew. That's the

thing about old friends; they know you better than anyone else.

You were wearing red in your live stream, so I thought something was up.

She's right, something is up. I never wear red on TV. It makes me look sick and is subtly polarizing to audiences. I'm about to leverage my hard-won position to blow up the modern media's hold on the imaginations of our citizens everywhere. Why did she have to pick today to watch my live stream? From the West Coast, no less? Oh, right, she had another baby. She was probably up with her.

I can swap it on camera, nbd. You know the clothes are never what I'm actually wearing. So how's little Maya this morning?

I put my phone face down so her response wouldn't interrupt me. She had busted me right before my big moment. I knew I could trust her not to say anything. Who would she tell, anyway? She knew more than she let on about what I was up to, the life I had built, and what I was about to do. But no one would ever question or tie anything I do back to her. We used different names when we met in that old Studio City theater.

We were both looking to break into Hollywood. She'd grown up in Topanga Canyon and had no strong ties to the industry, being a first-gen Angeleno. I'd flown out from Pennsylvania with big dreams and a young lifetime of memories I was looking forward to leaving behind. We bonded instantly in that character workshop. She helped me stop using my hands so much when I talked, and I helped her neutralize that valley rise in her voice.

Today my senator was going to miss an interview and had convinced the national network to let me take her place. This was a panel with the senator, the spokesman from Motto—one of the largest tech and social platforms on the planet—and an attorney from Peanut, a hardware company with a nearly 40 percent global market share—including the phone that buzzed on my desk.

I picked it up, and it was a message from my senator.

Thanks for sitting in today. – B

She might never speak to me again after this. She might blame me for her subsequent campaign loss and then for the rest of her life. I didn't care. It was long past time, and this was the perfect moment. I'd borrowed a video-switcher panel from the Senate's media center a while back and spent weeks programming it and customizing it for today. But, of course, I didn't know when today would come back then. Only that I was going to be ready when it did. I also set up a streaming deck to be live online before, during, and after the interview —and, most importantly, if my feed got cut by the network. I'd built my studio set in my living room, which also served as my bedroom, office, dining room, and kitchen.

Living in DC with a Hill staffer salary was mainly for those who had someone else paying the bills. I supplemented my English basement lifestyle by renting out my only bedroom to another Hill staffer, Jacinda White, from Atlanta. She's a legislative aide for her local congressman, on a year-long hiatus before law school. Jacinda was recently on *The Hill*'s "50 Most Beautiful People" list. She is beautiful, don't get me wrong. But that the list exists, and that she was willing to go through with it, has me scratching my head. Anything for a little bump in recognition, I guess. We've got to do everything we can to keep climbing, and it's no secret that when we say "everything," we mean it.

No problem! I responded to my boss.

I turned on my live stream on my tablet and got myself a glass of water. The fear of losing my voice has always haunted me, even in my dreams. Whenever I start my live streams, I turn them on and keep getting ready. I don't bother talking directly to the live audience when it starts. That's when the algorithm finds the right people and notifies them I'm live. My audience is not massive, just a couple hundred thousand followers, but it's enough to get the job done. Today, I was going live on two platforms to ensure I have a backup plan. I could see my viewer counts ticking up, so I waved to the camera as I got on my stool.

"Hi, guys! I'm about to go live on CBN, sitting in for the senator. I'm getting all set up right now."

I attached my lavalier mic to my necklace and tucked in my shirt nice and tight. I pushed my hair back behind my shoulders and stretched the top of my head toward the ceiling.

Jacinda rolled around the corner in her pajamas with her sleep mask on her forehead. The live stream audience to my right could see her, but the one to my left could not. The viewers started commenting about it, and I saw the audience move from one platform to another to get a glimpse of her. Some days, she hams it up in the background of my live streams, so my audience loves her. It turns out she wasn't in the mood to be the star of the show today. Instead, she rolled back into the hallway and shuffled back to the bedroom.

"We're not live yet, but I want to clue you guys in to something you'll see on TV today. You all can see that I'm in my apartment. That was my roommate, who many of you have met before. I live in this... um... lovely English basement apartment just steps from Capitol Hill."

I leaned forward to the tablet on my left, trying to pull the audience back to that platform, and held my hand up like I was telling them a secret.

"It's tiny. Like, really tiny. This room here is my bedroom, den, dining room, and kitchen. See that little window back there?"

I picked up the device and walked with it. Unfortunately,

the whispering didn't work, but taking the camera with me usually did the trick.

"That's the shared courtyard that all units have access to. I'm no expert on 'code,' but I'm sure this window isn't up to it. Do you think I could fit through there in an emergency?"

I laughed and saw the comments rolling in. People from all over the country watched my live streams, where I talked about what it was like to live and work on the Hill. This was my attempt to show people that not all of DC was a swamp in need of draining. That there were hard-working young people just like them getting paid next to nothing to do the actual work. Of course, I left out the scandalous parts and all the spin I did as part of my actual job. But one thing people could never get enough of was my living underground in this tiny apartment.

I turned around quickly when I heard the show go to a commercial break.

"That window over there, I think I can fit through that one! They dug down the steps below street level to get in, so it actually gets some light, too! It's also where the rats are, so see if you spot one!"

A little joke to keep them engaged while I put the device back on its stand.

"Okay, this is what's about to happen. I know you love my apartment—because it's so cute and cozy."

The comments blew up with "Jacinda!", "No, we love Jacinda!", "The hot roommate!", and I laughed.

"Yeah, yeah, I know. So, today I'm sitting in on this interview, and I thought, what if we did something a little different? What if I filmed it, like, in front of the White House lawn? Or with me sitting on Abraham Lincoln's lap?"

My comments blew up again. I checked the second platform, and the same thing was happening there.

"Film from the Oval Office!" one user said. "Metro,"

another said simultaneously. The responses were coming in so fast. I wanted to acknowledge the engagement, but it was more than I anticipated.

The view count started to rise.

My earpiece chirped. "We're live in fifteen, get ready," the TV producer said in my ear. I put my hand over my earpiece and nodded.

"Okay, friends. They just said we'd be going live in fifteen seconds. So be sure to watch this both here and on CBN— you can stream it. Don't miss anything!"

I hopped on my Peanut account, turned the live stream on, and put my phone beside my computer camera that was streaming to the network. I've been live so often that I can load the app and stream in seconds. Which was all I had left.

I held up my hand and showed the tablet on my left and the extra laptop on my right that we had five seconds left. I counted down as the earpiece perked up again with "We're live in five, four, three..."

A message from Adriana popped onto my screen.

I quickly flicked it away.

Olivia Kim, a former partisan political pundit turned business and tech reporter, opened the segment with her strong and halting voice.

"The antitrust bill currently in the Senate has failed to pass three times, but the bipartisan committee keeps bringing it back, hoping that some minor change will finally get them the signers they need to make it a reality. Joining us today is a panel of experts, and sitting in for the senator herself is her press secretary, Anna Kinlow. Thank you all for joining us."

"Thanks for having me, Olivia," piped Ben Walter, also a former political pundit, now head of public affairs of Motto.

I glanced at my phone just off camera, a knowing look to an audience that was growing past 10K viewers. My audience knows how I feel about Motto—the love/hate relationship I have with having to use their platform to best communicate with the people who elected my boss but also knowing how deeply intertwined the political and tech worlds are. I always felt like I was being permitted to take up space on Motto's app—the one I was streaming off my phone—because not letting me ramble would amount to censorship. They were clearly not going to take a stance on that lest it meant they would have to do it more universally.

I shifted in my seat while Olivia lobbed the first question to Dianne Michaels, the attorney from Peanut. When she did, I glanced at the extra laptop streaming to Peanut's platform. Peanut and Motto were both named in the antitrust bill my boss was reworking in the Senate. I was essentially here to hold their feet to the fire. One way I did that was by also streaming on the Indian-owned platform Bloom. What had started as a platform strictly built for beauty bloggers— and, to be clear, I was never one of those—turned into a massive network that has a majority of young women users compared to other platforms. We all know that's where the global spending power is. My Bloom stream was sitting at 107K viewers. That was relatively high for me, especially for a Tuesday morning.

"And that's why we think, again, Senator Gardner's bill won't pass. It's time for her to move on and focus on things that matter to the people who elected her, like Medicare and Social Security."

My Motto audience responded with comments like "yes!" and "preach!"

I subtly moved my hand, reached for the streaming deck, and pressed the big green button. On the CBN stream, my background changed to a fake DC backdrop as if I were filming from the balcony of the Senate with the Washington Monument in the background. My shirt changed from a red fitted T-shirt to a white button-up top with a delicate Peter Pan collar with kelly green piping. My hair darkened, and a flattering pink lipstick adorned my lips.

"What the hell are you doing?" the producer yelled in my ear. "I'll cut your feed if you do that again."

"What do you think, Anna?" Olivia asked me with a stoic look, pretending like she had no idea about what I'd just done. "Do you think the bill will pass this time? Or should the Senate direct their attention elsewhere?"

The question allowed me to shift in my chair again, and I peeked at the streaming numbers on each side. I had 115K on Bloom, and the Peanut channel was up to 25K. Both were climbing.

"In her role as Senate Majority Leader and Chair of the Senate Judiciary Subcommittee on Competition Policy, Senator Gardner's focus on antitrust is, in fact, the most representative of the will of the people who elected her. With only the four of us here right now, we are controlling the media narrative directed at over two-thirds of the country, not to mention our global audiences," I started.

"But, Anna, how will breaking up Peanut or Motto help Americans afford the healthcare they need?" Olivia pressed.

"Breaking up Peanut and Motto, disassembling them into the multitudes of parts they have accumulated through the past decade using revenue generated off the data of individual users, will have numerous effects on the tech industry, business, and even how everyday Americans consume media and spend their money."

"That's a reach, Anna," Ben interjected.

"I have to agree with Ben," Olivia started. "And when we return, we'll see what Peanut thinks about that." Olivia gave the camera a look of intensity, and we rolled into the commercial break.

The hum in my earpiece went dead—they cut my feed

during the break, probably to talk about my background change. So I turned to the Bloom audience.

"What do you think?" I asked, watching the comments roll in.

"How did you change your outfit on camera?"

"I hate watching the news."

"Uh, I hate Olivia Kim."

"Ben Walter sucks!!"

"take ur shirt off."

"Right?!" I responded to nothing in particular. I glanced over at the Peanut audience, having jumped to 234K viewers.

"I have another little segment before they move on to the latest Elon scandal. Any tips?" I asked to the Peanut camera.

I grabbed my phone off its stand, forgetting the Motto audience was there. I pulled down my notifications from the top, letting the camera continue to stream. The Motto audience didn't interest me as it skewed older and was generally more unhinged. The message from Adriana was still sitting there.

Think twice before whatever you're about to do.

That was from five minutes ago, right before we went live. I thought back to the many times she'd seen me calculate an implosion of my life. From the diner we both worked at and I walked out on, to the nice guy who was boring me to death, to my job at the start-up that led to a sealed settlement and a fresh start on the East Coast. I'd thought twice about all of those. And looking back, I still have no regrets.

I flipped back to Motto and spoke to the only person watching who I cared about.

"Keep watching." I smiled and replaced the phone on its stand.

The hum in my ear returned, and CBN's producer was talking, but not to me. "Okay, folks, we're coming back in five, four..."

I spun back straight in my seat.

I reached down and tapped the purple button on the streaming deck.

I looked straight at the camera and smiled.

"And we're back, oh..." started Olivia, touching her ear. "Yes, wow, thank you for joining us, Senator Gardner."

I nodded and curled my lips ever so slightly, just the way she does. I watched as Ben and Dianne shifted in their chairs.

"Before the break, we discussed with Anna the ultimate benefits of antitrust action against Motto and Peanut. Do you have anything to add?"

I paused and thought for a moment.

"Anna explained it clearly," I started slowly, channeling her vocal cadence. I glanced at the Peanut stream, which had jumped again to 508K viewers. "Without competition, where are our checks and balances? The business portfolios of Peanut and Motto have given them outsized market control at the great expense of everyday Americans. By maintaining the status quo, that being endless acquisitions and, let's say, devouring the entirety of the data available on every user watching right now and selling it for their financial gain, what safeguard do we have from their total manipulation of all content? And sorry, Olivia, to point this out—we all know that more content is consumed online than on TV..."

Olivia continued to stare at me with a stern face without acknowledging what I'd just said.

"Olivia, if I may," Dianne interrupted at the perfect time.

Olivia nodded and touched her ear.

Dianne started into her talking points about the unfairness of M&A review, but my eyes locked on Olivia. She picked up her tablet from her desk and looked down while Dianne talked. I had to guess which platform she was just tipped off to, and I thought it was probably Peanut.

I turned and winked at the Peanut audience, and Olivia dropped the tablet on her table.

"Dianne, sorry to interrupt you. Senator Gardner."

I looked up at the camera.

"Or should we say 'Anna'?"

In my ear, the producer was back. "Don't you ever show your face in this town again." The connection was dead. I saw my space on CBN go black.

"Looks like we've lost Senator Gardner."

I let out a sigh of relief.

"Whew!" I said, pulling my hair back into a quick bun at my nape. I turned to my Bloom audience. "That was wild, right? I have a feeling my Motto and Peanut audiences..." I started as my Motto stream dropped. So I looked at my Peanut audience.

"Welp, Motto is gone, but you're all still here—for now. If we get cut off, I'm always live on—" My Peanut stream was cut. I turned back to my Bloom stream.

"We're still live, right?" I asked.

EXPECTATION

"What are you gonna tell them this time?" Avyan asked as Hunter arrived late for the weekly research team meeting.

"I'll tell them I was reorganizing the supply closet because it looked like a hurricane hit it," Hunter replied, putting his satchel down and sitting with his friend in the small auditorium where he and his colleagues met weekly to discuss their latest findings, but only after they heard an update from someone outside of their lab. "Fifty bucks says this guy references research at least two years old."

"You know I'm not taking that bet," Avyan said.

They both smiled a knowing grin and looked toward the front, where a representative from Kragin Edström, a pharmaceutical juggernaut, explained their latest development in acute pain management.

"Why do they waste our time with this industry bullshit?" Hunter whispered, sliding down in his seat and leaning on his hand. Their boss, Dr. Marie Nova, glanced at them in a way that showed she was officially annoyed but not yet angry about their interruptions.

"She wouldn't look at you like that if you'd just publish already," Avyan whispered to Hunter.

Hunter gritted his teeth, withholding his comment about how she was probably more disappointed that Avyan hadn't tried to sleep with her like every other woman at the lab, mostly because he couldn't be entirely sure of its accuracy. He sighed instead and twirled his wedding band, a new soothing habit he'd developed to remind himself he'd done at least one thing he planned to do before he was thirty. If you'd asked anyone he worked with, he'd picked the wrong goal to focus on for his research. He just let them think what they wanted.

"Dr. Lynch," Dr. Nova called to Hunter as the presenter left the lectern. Hunter stood up and picked up his satchel. He put the old bag in the chair he was previously sitting in and unlatched the front buckles to reveal a bag full of curled paper of various colors and groupings. "Dr. Lynch, are you still planning to present an update on your research today?" Dr. Nova asked, sounding like she was moving up that anger scale. Hunter heard snickers from his coworkers. He glanced at Avyan, who gave him a big fake smile and a thumbs-up.

"Yes, I am," Hunter replied, carrying a creased, stained folder to the lectern. The pharmaceutical representative lingered in the doorway, and Hunter stared at him, letting him know he would not start until the man had left—Hunter's work was proprietary after all. The man left, along with two senior researchers. Hunter looked back at his folder and then up at his audience. He glanced down again at the paper-clipped photo of his wife, Lily, at the top of the patient profile.

"As many of you know, my research focuses on germ line editing, hoping we can one day offer this as a supplementary service to our clients," Hunter started.

"Dude, we know. It's been the same thing for five years. Boy genius does one thing right and takes forever to develop a new idea," yelled out Gary, who unfortunately shared a lab with Hunter.

"Dr. Stephens, decorum," Dr. Nova said to Gary.

"Yes, it has, Gary, and you'll be pleased to know that we will see the results of my new hypothesis in the coming weeks. We've successfully tracked the gene development in a live fetus with no notable negative developments for the fetus or mother. In short, the testing of the targeting mechanism hypothesis is going well."

Gary slow-clapped three times, stood up, and left the room. A few others quietly left behind him, leaving Dr. Nova, Avyan, a few new interns, and Hunter's intern, Jamaica.

"That's wonderful news, Hunter," Dr. Nova said as she started packing her own bag. She turned away but quickly turned back with her eyebrow raised, a detail that sent a slight panic directly into Hunter's chest. "I assume you're keeping Legal and Ethics looped in. Do you have anything we can share publicly yet?" Dr. Nova asked.

"Not yet, but soon," Hunter said with relief to know somewhere inside of her business-is-everything exterior, Dr. Nova was still curious about the details of his work. She had always shown that she believed in him, giving him an extra-long leash to work around the fringes of his capabilities. It was Dr. Nova who ultimately granted him access to build his custom AI gene editor in the lab setting, despite the arguments from his peers like Gary, who thought that AI's influence on gene editing would ultimately lead to humanity's demise. She encouraged him to keep going when he took longer than his peers to deliver developments that would help keep the lights on. She never spoke to him about why she seemed to believe in him or his acutely specific and personal germ line editing goals, and she didn't ask too many questions that might have led him to disclose some questionable or illegal activity. For all the faith she seemed to have in him, he was infinitely more self-motivated.

"Well, keep us posted." Dr. Nova dropped her eyebrow

and smiled with tightly pressed lips before gathering her things and heading toward the door.

"Will do," Hunter replied, closing his folder and taking it with him.

Avyan's most recent conquest slid into Hunter's seat, not seeing his bag, and whispered something in Avyan's ear just as Hunter returned to their row. She stopped whispering and turned toward Hunter, visibly annoyed by the interruption.

"I think you're..." Hunter said, pointing to her miniskirt. Her eyes widened, her lips parted, and she looked at Avyan. "You're sitting on my bag!" Hunter said quickly to stop her reaction in real time. He changed how he was pointing to show that he was pointing around her and not at any specific body part. She scoffed at him, stood up, straightened her miniskirt, and left the chair, walking down the aisle the other way. Avyan watched, looking at Hunter with a smile on his face. She looked back at Avyan, and his face changed.

"Dude, what's your problem?" he asked Hunter.

"I don't have a problem. I just needed to get my bag, and she was basically lying on it. You guys really need to get a room. Keep this stuff out of the office before you get tangled up in some kind of policy violation."

"Why do we need a room? We're just two colleagues enjoying a collegial debate with the perfect amount of scientific rigor," Avyan said, rising from his seat and gesticulating an act that should, in fact, get a room. "And I don't think you're the guy to warn me about policy violations. I'm not the one editing the genes of an unborn child and hiding it from everyone around me," Avyan said semi-seriously as he stood up and followed the miniskirt. "Jamaica," he said flatly to the woman who had walked up behind Hunter.

"Yes?" Jamaica responded flatly, mocking his tone.

"I knew you'd say yes one day, girl!" Avyan responded with a laugh.

Hunter and Jamaica both audibly sighed.

"Okay, okay, I'll get out of your way," Avyan said, looking around for the long-gone intern.

"Dr. Lynch," Jamaica started. Her black-rimmed glasses sat low on her nose. She carried three textbooks in front of her chest. Her long braids featured an interwoven red streak on the right side. "What policy violations was he talking about? Have you made progress that I don't know about? You know, I'm here to support you and your work, but the last I checked, you weren't weeks away from finishing anything new. And I know your wife is due to deliver soon, which means you'll be out with her and the new baby, and you haven't given me anything I can keep going in your absence."

"I know, I know. Don't take this the wrong way, but this is why I work alone. I want to be able to follow my ideas and not get bogged down when a new one comes up. I don't like to have to—"

"Explain your work, I know," Jamaica cut him off. "But you have to write things down—or even just say words, and I'll write them down—if you want me to work on them," Jamaica responded. They moved toward the double door of the entrance, and Hunter opened the door for her. Jamaica smiled and pushed her glasses up the bridge of her nose.

"I know. I've been working on that. Look, I promise to share some notes with you soon," Hunter replied with a kind smile.

His phone buzzed in his pocket. It was a text from his father. He put his phone back in his pocket, put the weathered folder back in his satchel, and looped the long strap across his chest. Hunter smiled at Jamaica again as he broke away down a different hall and headed toward the vending machines. Jamaica sighed and changed course, following him at a distance—the way she had found worked best.

Jamaica was at the top of her class and knew working for

Dr. Hunter Lynch would be much more complicated than any academic challenge. But she weighed the potential outcomes and calculated that even being associated with the scientist who had first begun editing virus DNA with AI-led recommendations would be exciting and groundbreaking. In her three months since joining Dr. Lynch's team, if you could call it that, she'd had more time to test her own hypotheses and study Dr. Lynch since he never seemed interested in looping her in on his work.

He spent long, quiet hours alone in his office and lab, typing to his personal AI that he hosted offline in the lab and running experiments on mice. With his early germ line editing, he'd made mice stronger, capable of building 15 percent more muscle. This idea didn't excite him nearly as much as his employer, but the work bought him endless resources and patience from his boss. In fact, Jamaica's grant existed as part of the award for his work. He wasn't interested in an assistant, so Dr. Nova did the interview and placed Jamaica on his team.

Jamaica walked by his office door as Hunter signed to the camera on the stand on his desk, "How much blood?" with a concentrated look on his face. He saw her watching him and motioned for her to come in.

"It's Lily," he said to Jamaica, "close the door." He turned back to his dad and signed, "My assistant is here. I have to go. I will leave in five minutes." He disconnected the call.

Jamaica asked, "Is she okay?" but did not respond to the signs since they weren't meant for her. She felt a pang of anxiety in the pit of her stomach. She had also taught herself to read sign language while she waited on Dr. Lynch to find a use for her, and it seemed like today it would finally pay off. Learning to read his signs felt like an invasion of his privacy, but it was also how she found out that he was experimenting on his unborn child and he was doing it to prevent the genetic deafness that his father lived with.

"Please come around to this side," Hunter said to her. Spilling piles of papers, notebooks, and scientific journals took up all the flat areas of his desk. He used two large curved monitors to display this computer-based work.

Jamaica walked around the edge of his desk and looked at his screens. She was glad he wasn't looking at her face when she first glimpsed the screens. Unlike his desk and general demeanor, the desktop of the dual-screen setup was meticulous. She could see his calendar, which was small in the upper-left corner. Under it was a running note of details with what appeared to be daily assessments of the medical symptoms of his study patient. Next to those, she saw a visualization of the double helix and quickly identified the GJB2 gene, which encoded the connexin 26 (Cx26) protein. This was the gene mechanism that caused most autosomal recessive deafness in humans.

"Hunter," Jamaica started. She had never referred to him by anything other than Dr. Lynch. Her heart was pounding in her ears. Tears welled in the bottom of her eyelids.

"There's too much to explain now," he replied.

"I don't need an explanation," she breathed, moving closer to his chair, her hands trembling. "But this is..."

"It's remarkable, I know. I'm going to change the future of humanity."

"No, it's this other mutation here," Jamaica said, pointing to the screen with a trembling finger.

"I've reviewed every single protein that matters. I can't teach you right now," Hunter said curtly.

"I don't need you to teach me," Jamaica signed to him. A tear ran down her cheek.

Hunter paused, searching her eyes, trying to remember

everything he had signed in front of her, thinking she couldn't understand. He didn't know how he had offended her and didn't have the patience to figure it out.

"Look, I have to go. Lily is at Memorial Hospital. Review everything here and be on call for me to reach out," Hunter said, standing and grabbing his satchel. He looked at his desk again and decided on a stack of papers and a notebook to take with him, sliding them inside. He opened the door and turned back. "Thank you, Jamaica. And obviously, let's keep this between us for now."

He opened his office door and turned back to see Jamaica in his chair. Hunter looked down at the folder with the creases, coffee rings, and tattered pages. He pulled it out of his arm and placed it on the table inside the door.

Avyan opened Hunter's door as he was pushing his back through it. Hunter fell back with the quick release of the door's tension.

"Whoa there, tiger," Avyan said, catching Hunter's arm. The folder fell to the hallway floor and landed wide open, and Avyan saw Lily's photo and the ultrasounds of their child. Avyan and Hunter stared at each other as Avyan connected the dots while Hunter tried to pick them up and undo what had just happened. Avyan searched Hunter's eyes for an answer and came up with nothing. "I wondered why you were so secretive about it. I honestly thought you were having an affair with your patient."

"That's not funny. You need to stay away from this," Hunter said, pointing to his folder.

Avyan threw his hands in the air. "I have no intention of getting anywhere near that mess. You've broken so many ethics and laws here, bro."

Hunter hushed Avyan as other employees were approaching.

"For real, man. What were you thinking?" Avyan hissed.

"Breakthroughs take risks... bro," Hunter said with a demeaning tone. "While you're busy trying to get laid, I'm funding this entire place."

"You're going to get this whole place shut down. What the hell, man," Avyan replied as he stepped back.

"Or—I'm going to make history," Hunter said quietly as he stepped directly toward Avyan. "Again."

Avyan raised his chest and kept his feet still. He was a whole foot shorter than Hunter, but wasn't afraid to stand his ground. "Is this about you or her? Or better yet, the baby in there?" he spat, pointing to the folder.

"I have to go." Hunter brushed into Avyan, who turned to let him pass.

"Dude, that's your family," Avyan said to him as he walked away.

———

In the emergency room waiting area, Hunter found his father sitting, looking at his phone with his reading glasses balanced on the tip of his nose. He walked directly toward him and caught his father's eye. When they made eye contact, Hunter's heart dropped.

"Tell me," Hunter signed to his father.

"I don't know much. They're waiting for you. They just told me she's fighting hard," his father signed back.

"What do you mean? Fighting the staff?" Hunter signed back.

"For her life."

"Baby?"

His father's eyes pooled with tears, and his lip trembled. Hunter collapsed into the chair beside his father and drew his hands to his face. He pulled out his phone and opened an interface with his AI. He entered:

<< Status update: Fetus 3 failed today. >>

<< LAB-BOT: Updating memory. >>

"Are you Mr. Lynch?" a nurse asked him, interrupting as he typed another response.

"We both are," Hunter signed and voiced to her. She smiled politely.

"We'd like to bring you back," the nurse replied, her arms gesturing to Hunter.

"Okay, I'll go," Hunter signed and said again. He looked at his father. His father reached out and grasped Hunter's hand and squeezed it before letting it drop.

"I'll be right here," his father signed.

Hunter followed the nurse to the patient care area. She led him past multiple beds separated by curtains and to a door, a private room. Through the door window, he could see Lily motionless on the bed, a ventilator attached to her face, a bump still on her torso.

"She's not awake right now. You're welcome to go in and sit with her. Dr. Wakefield will be by to speak with you."

Hunter swallowed and pushed into the room, trying to take in as much data as he could to assess her condition. He got out his phone, took pictures of her IV bag and monitor stats, and entered more notes into his app.

———

"They were buried together," his father signed through the glass.

"That's good," Hunter signed back with tears in his eyes.

"Some of your old colleagues came to the service. It was nice to finally meet the people you spent so much time with. And your assistant, Jamaica, she can sign!"

Hunter nodded, thinking about how Jamaica had agreed to take over his research while he served his sentence for involuntary manslaughter. His lab-provided attorneys got the charges for practicing medicine without a license and violation of human research ethics laws dropped, which meant his sentence shrunk dramatically and he would likely only serve eighteen months in prison.

"I've had a good life, son," his father signed. "I wouldn't change anything. Anything!" he emphasized.

Hunter took a deep breath through his nose and let it out before signing, "I know, Dad." His eyes were soft like those of a boy. "I just thought if I could give him a chance to live a normal..."

"I am normal!" his father signed back and slammed his open palm on the table in front of him.

"You know what I mean, Dad," Hunter signed back. He ran his fingers through his hair in frustration. "Like, easier," he added.

"I don't think you understand something fundamental here. Humans aren't some code to perfect. And life, as you now know, is fragile and sacred. You can't 'genius' your way out of prison."

"There are laws created by humans and laws created by nature. We were given ears so that we could hear," Hunter signed back.

"No one can hear who isn't willing to listen," his father signed.

Hunter looked away.

His father rapped on the window to pull him back. He continued, "Your brilliance is nothing without a heart. All the awards and money won't bring them back. Don't you see?"

"I think that this was so close. The breakthroughs here are world-changing," Hunter signed.

"None of that matters in the end," his father signed, his cheeks wet with tears. "I love you dearly, son." He stood up and touched the glass with his hand, his arthritic fingers unable to fully extend. Then he turned and pushed the button to leave.

Hunter watched his father's back as he waited for a guard to let him out. He lifted his hand and touched where his father's had been on the glass, then he punched the glass.

"We were so close," he said to himself.

TERMINAL

I used to wake up and wonder what tragedy that day would bring. I'm not a pessimist, you see, but life has given me more and more reasons to feel that way.

Today, and every day since I was moved in here, I woke up and thought I'd journeyed on. That I was about to meet the Big Man. Or Woman. Or maybe it's not so binary. I'm not even a religious person. My parents forced me to go to Sunday School, and I mostly played tic-tac-toe on the pamphlet during the main service. But I made sure I didn't force that on my kids when they were young. Still, when you get old and feel like everyone and everything around you is a countdown clock, you have to figure out some way to squash the anxiety of what comes next. Even those of us who may be feeling a little tired of all of this humanness are a bit apprehensive from time to time.

"Good morning, Evelyn," the voice said to me in its calm and neutral way.

I was still floating inside the dream of a marsh. My husband and I had taken the kids to the Everglades when people still did that. The part about the parrot appearing to have a conversation with my daughter, who was only five at the time, about the benefits of regularly practicing calisthenics, however—and unfortunately, if you think about it—never happened. I could still feel the burning touch of the Florida sun on the backs of my shoulders. I was hot but liked it, even if I knew I wasn't supposed to say it since the entire planet was burning itself alive. It still is, mind you. All these years later. And we're still here pretending everything is normal.

Slowly, the heat gave way to softness and then to cool, and in an instant, they were all gone. Again. That bitter taste in the morning was more sour on days like these.

"Were you dreaming of your family again?" the voice asked.

I used to lie whenever it asked me things I didn't want to face, share, or think about another moment. I argued to myself that my inner life belonged to me, and sharing it would both create more pain and somehow give them ammunition in their power over me. It doesn't matter that I'm ninety-eight years old; if I think I can somehow stick it to the man or a thing created by man, I'm gonna try it at least once. That's something they'll never be able to take away from me. But on this topic, I have since relented and begun to share more of my inner world with the voice. Despite my own hesitations about doing so and my reluctance to never tell it this in any straightforward way, it seems to have helped.

My whole life, I thought that when you get old, people around you drop like flies. We each lose some good ones along the way and learn what grief really feels like, but ultimately, it's you or them, and everyone's gonna go, eventually. Horrible as it sounds, it seemed the generations before me just bore the losses piling up with some weathered grit they developed over their lifetimes. When my circle started shrinking, the pain became physical. So I did what any retiree with nothing but time and free healthcare would do—I got physical therapy!

My bed began moving, and the electric blinds rose on the window to my left.

"I'd like to be in Florida—the Everglades," I said before I opened my eyes. This was a little trick I did for myself. It gave the voice time to load my window with the right environment. While it could assess everything from my heart rate to my bowel movements, I tried to keep this one request unpredictable. I'm probably failing at that. I know it can read my dreams while I sleep. Did I pick the Everglades yesterday? I don't want to know. It's better if I don't focus on that and stay focused on the present. You know how they say today is a gift and all that? Well, it sounds like horseshit, but it's where I am these days.

My weight shifted to my hips as the gentle motor in the bed got me upright. The shift shook free a cough, but the fit ended quickly. I've woken up with hip and back pain for years that turned into decades. A new mattress has never helped. But somehow, this place has. I feel like I'm in my seventies again!

What I would give to actually be in my seventies again. Not for my health or mobility, but just to walk the earth with them again. I don't know who I miss the most sometimes. You're never supposed to say you have a favorite when you have kids. I never did, anyway. When your whole family is gone, the conflict feels similar. You wish you could tell your husband about some arcane thing that adds a new beat to a multi-decade narrative only you two share. You wish you could hear a laugh or stroke a cheek. Being the last one standing—or in my case, riding an electrified bed—feels more like a sentence to serve than any physical victory.

I heard birds and sensed the light shifting to a warmer hue. I opened my eyes and glanced toward the window to see green, lush, and waving. An egret stood near a marshy edge, poking at the ground.

"Thank you," I said. Ever since they've become more integrated into our lives, I've had this deep fear of them judging me and taking out some sort of retribution if I'm ever unkind. I know the protocols are in place—I helped develop them—but that's exactly why I don't fully trust them. When you see how the sausage is made, kind of thing.

"You're welcome, Evelyn. Do you need assistance standing today?"

Out of my wall, parts extended until they fully moved away and formed a three-sided walker with chunky, jagged wheels on the bottom. The handles that rose toward my bed were rippled and squishy for an easier, nonslip grip. I swung my legs toward the device and shifted my weight to the floor without gripping the handles. I knew I'd need them, but I liked to see how I'd fare until I did. In my mind, it was also calculating my reaction time and dependency per square inch as it was charting my demise. That's how I would have designed it, anyway.

The bones in my feet compressed into the floor. My weight shifted to my toes, and I gripped hard to slow the pendulum swing of the rest of me. I straightened my back and rose to my full height, now a towering 5′1″. My weight balanced between both feet. It was tempting to stretch my arms above my head, but as soon as I arched my back and raised my hands, the room spun quickly, and I found my hands on the padded grips. Accepting defeat, I held on tight and stretched my back a bit more. I studied the device in front of me and thought it might have been more interesting had a face-like feature been included on a panel in the bar. Humans need to see faces to connect. Even babies know this. However, after the humanoid robots caused such a divisive response in society, developers moved away from these designs when they were unnecessary.

I shuffled my bare feet toward the bathroom, the robotic

walker guiding me there. The bathroom floor was warm, and the air was aromatic and moist. Eucalyptus. The walker took me to the toilet and then to the sink. There, I got a glimpse in the mirror.

"Would you like to schedule a haircut today?" Voice asked.

Something seemed off in my appearance. I'd assumed it was the shock of my aged look. I swear, just yesterday, I didn't have so many spots, my hair was twice as thick, and my eyes looked less likely to close forever.

"No, I'm going to grow it out," I lied. And it knew I lied, and I didn't care. Lying to it didn't fall into the being-unkind bucket. It shouldn't have been reading my mind, anyway.

I splashed water on my face and washed it with a milky rose-scented soap. My walker positioned itself behind me and lowered a seat for me to take if needed, which I didn't, thank you. After completing my morning routine, my walker and I returned to my room. My bed was gone, and a couch was in its place. This automated change was soundless. Even the light temperature and radiance mimicked the progression of the sun. My workout clothes and slip-on sneakers were on the couch, since I usually work out first thing in the morning.

I gripped my walker and turned it to the right, to my cabinet in the wall. As I approached it, it opened, and inside, I saw everything I ever loved. I reached out and touched the framed photo of my boys, a sculpture made of clay, and a wedding photo. There was a photo of the family in the Everglades where some random little girl had snuck into the framing beside my eldest son and smiled at the camera as if she were joining our family vacation. A pen holder painted with what could generously be described as abstract floral art on the outside held long-dried and irrelevant pens. The warm wood inside this cabinet gave off the slightest smell of home.

———

"How is she doing today?"

"Her vitals are stable," her device responded.

"Has she left the room yet?" Allison asked.

"No."

Allison sighed and took a sip of ginger tea. She sat at her home in the mountains, overlooking the fog that rose from the valley below. Her husband, Patrick, walked into the living room and saw her facing the window.

"I'm going for a hike with Michael. We have our beacons. The AQI is only one-eighty today, so I'll probably start without my mask. Michael said visibility at Hawk's View is nearly a mile. Should be back in about four hours." Patrick stopped, realizing Allison wasn't listening to him.

"I don't think it's going to work," Allison replied.

Patrick put his water bottle on the dining table and walked to Allison. He sat on the couch beside her chair. Allison placed her teacup on the saucer and put them on the side table. She swiveled her chair back toward him.

"It's been four months, P."

"I know."

"They said memory recovery validation takes three."

"That's the average."

"Yesterday, she asked them to 'remove that random child from the family picture.' I'm her daughter. And all she has left. How could she forget that? Should we just bring her back here?" Allison asked, already knowing the answer.

"You know that wouldn't work. It was way more than you and I could handle last time. Plus, they know now. She's already on the list. This at least gives her a chance. Plus, it's the most civilized way."

"Maybe we get an assistant or build her a recovery box inside the guest room?"

"Honey. You know we can't change course now. Don't you

think, of everyone you know, your mom has the best chance of pulling through this? She literally helped design the place."

"They're going to terminate her. They don't care. They're following the protocol. She's going to die. There. We'll never see her again," Allison said, tears finally breaching her lower lids, leaving a streak under each eye that caught the light from the lamp on the table.

"Everyone goes eventually. I think she likes the experimental nature. Well, she would if she remembered who she was," Patrick said quietly while looking at the floor.

Allison picked up her tea and turned back to the fog.

———

When they brought me here, I woke up on a stretcher, and they gave me a cozy sleep mask. They don't know it, but they put it on sloppy, and I could peek out of the nose area. I mean, can you imagine? One minute, I'm living a completely normal life; the next minute, I'm waking up on a gurney in the desert. Yes, the desert. I didn't live anywhere near a desert before. I lived somewhere with real trees, that's for sure. Never wanted to spend any time in this part of the country. I assume I haven't left the country.

I never felt the heat, but I saw through the windows of the docking area. It wasn't like these fake windows. It was the real outside. I felt the air but, luckily, never the direct heat. I guess they flew me here because how else would I have gotten all the way to this hellhole?

Before the sudden change in scenery, I was doing fine. Or so I thought. Being here is making me rethink that. Once I realized they would not kill me immediately or harvest my organs while I was awake (who would?), I understood I needed to stay healthy and try to outlive this situation. If there's one thing I'm good at, it's outliving. I've outlived things, people, plants, and even cities, come to think of it.

The quaint little town I was born in is long gone. Completely abandoned by civilization. Remains of roads and shadows of bridges are there, but no one lives as part of any community. When the heat got so bad, it brought tornadoes, and people slowly got the message and headed to new pastures. A pathetic Rome.

Once, my Johnny and I took the boys there to show it to them, and it damn near killed me. The memories I had of being a kid at that daycare, of playing on that hill, of swimming in that pool—now it looked like it had suffered through a militant invasion. Skeletons of swing sets, trees bursting through the sidewalk with evidence of burns. I never went back again—figured it was nicer in my memories.

"I've changed my mind," I called out to Voice. "I think I will go to the salon today. I just want to walk by, though. See what it's all about."

"Very well. When would you like to go?" Voice replied.

I was still in my exercise suit and considered this momentarily before responding, "Can we go now?"

The walker rolled over to the bench I was sitting on. I grabbed the handles and hoisted myself to stand. For a second, I thought I must have gained back some muscle because it felt too easy. Then I felt the slightest pinch behind my left leg where the bench snagged my pants on its way back down. The light on the walker turned from red to green. The wheels were ready to roll, and so was I.

———

Allison and Patrick sat side by side on the screen, patiently waiting.

"You don't appear surprised. Most families have more

pronounced reactions to learning about escape attempts. I didn't see a documented history in her chart, but perhaps this isn't the first time?" Dr. Park asked.

Patrick and Allison glanced at each other.

"What I'm more interested in learning is why the treatments aren't working. This costs a fortune. We've read all the literature. We understood that her statistical chances were better than what we're seeing in action. What is going wrong here?" Allison asked, pleading.

"You understand that her attempt to escape violates the terms of the agreement?" Dr. Park responded. "Any violation of the terms requires us to report her to the Department of Resource Re-collection for immediate termination. You are well aware of our country's resource restraints. If you need further verification or education about this topic—"

"How can we use this episode to continue her progress? We have thirty-four days left, correct?" Allison cut her off.

Dr. Park removed her glasses and pushed her silky black hair behind her shoulder. She cleared her throat and folded her hands on the desk in front of her. Her movement appeared performative. Her hair was even more perfect in this new configuration and moved like a veil of silk.

"Please give her a little more time," Patrick asked, leaning closer to the camera. "We all saw that Alli was there in her dream. We know she's in there somewhere."

"Dreams do not validate association or familial relations," Dr. Park replied calmly.

"You know she's my mother; you've already done the DNA test!" Allison said, standing up and walking off camera.

"Yes, we confirmed you are biologically related. But her identity doesn't include you, and your brothers are deceased. Due to our limited resources, the government requires all citizens to have familial relations with other citizens to maintain their citizenship. Those without family and without notable contributions to society are placed on a path toward termination to reduce the burden of their existence, and their chemical compounds can provide the resources humanity needs to survive."

"No contributions!" Allison's voice echoed from another room. "Do you even know who you're talking about?"

"Are there any other treatment options—even experimental?" Patrick asked.

"The kinds of treatment she needs to reverse the damage don't bring back memories. Once they're gone, they're gone," Dr. Park responded.

"Let me see her," Allison said, her voice closer. Patrick turned and looked to where she was standing, knowing the answer and knowing Allison knew it, too.

Dr. Park continued, "I recommend assisted termination take place in our facility. We have a much more compassionate process than the department."

"Don't you think it's a bit early to discuss this?" Patrick asked, eyes darting off-screen. His hand rubbed his hairline.

"She's making progress," Allison said as she sat back in her chair, shaking her hair from her face.

"Please continue her treatment," Patrick added.

"The process can take up to fourteen days. It's a slow release, and they feel absolutely no pain. Our scans confirm this," Dr. Park responded.

"She remembers me," Allison said softly.

———

The walker got close to the doorway, and the door to my room slid open with a hiss. It led me over the threshold, and I slowly turned to the left. My sneakers squeaked on the floor. I felt a hard, bony hand reach up from my gut and grip my heart. My heart started beating faster, and the hand gripped harder. My heart was fighting to survive.

"You seem anxious. Would you like to sit?" Voice asked. I took a deep breath. It was annoying how much my vital signs tattled on me. Nothing was secret. Nothing was sacred.

"No, thank you. Let's keep going." I gave the walker a shove forward.

I didn't remember them pushing me down this hallway. Maybe we came in the other way. The walls were covered in wood grain. They reminded me of my dad's shed. Plywood. I swear I smelled that old shed. The wood dust and tools and collection of odds and ends. Dad had a habit of leaving pencils around the shed for marking and whatnot. Once, my neighbor Dani and I got the grand idea to use those pencils to scribble our names on the walls as many times as we could before our hands were stiff from writing.

Something caught my eye. I slowed down and looked low on the wall beside the front wheel. A series of hand-drawn flowers was on the wall. A heart with the words "Evelyn and Dani BFF." It was a weird coincidence, though I didn't know who Evelyn was.

I pushed my walker forward and released my hands from it. In a quick and athletic movement, I turned and ditched it, leaving it in my dust. At least that's how it felt. I wanted to move faster still, but knew I needed to get blood moving into my feet before I could sprint.

Glancing back, I saw the walker's wheels were slowing, tracking toward me, their high-tread friction gripping the tile floor with squeaks and grunts. My foot chirped as the heel of my shoe scuffed the floor. A handrail against the wall—was it there before?—provided the nudge I needed to right myself. The momentum inside me wound from my feet to my hips.

"Evelyn," Voice said calmly. That name again.

I could tell I was caught. Damn. I was so close that time.

The seat of the walker gently tapped the back of my knee. It rose against the back of my thigh until it was under my rear, offering me a seat. And at no better time, because that sprint took it out of me.

———

Dear Mr. and Mrs. Wilson,

I regret to inform you that Ms. Evelyn Rose Baker has violated the terms of the Memory Recall and Relations Retrieval agreement. Per our obligation to remain accredited, we have reported her to the Federal Expiration Registry, which notified the Department of Resource Re-collection. Per the agreement, she will receive compassionate termination within 14 days. You are permitted one virtual communication experience during this time. You will receive further notice to schedule your connection time. Please remember that when you communicate with her, the termination process will have already begun and will be irreversible. Thank you for your contribution of limited resources for actively contributing members of our society.

- Dr. Park

Patient Liaison

Memory Recovery and Validation, Inc.

———

"Evelyn, you have a communication opportunity today," Voice said.

"Is it optional?" I responded. Something had changed. I'd been on my routine, but I'd been sleeping more, and when I sleep, I dream. Much more than before. Then I wake up tired and cranky and want to go back to sleep.

"It is always within your control," Voice responded. I

didn't buy it. It wanted me to do this call. Just like when my mother used to act like things were up to me, but if I didn't pick what she wanted, she withheld her affection and even attention. I always said if I ever got to be a mother, especially to a girl, I wouldn't be that way. Life didn't give me the chance. My boy filled me up with joy, though. In the back of my mind, I always knew I could have loved more children, even despite my busy work life.

"Okay, when is it?" I asked.

"It is in one hour. Would you like to shower before you connect?" Voice asked. I didn't understand the point of that. I'd showered yesterday. Well, I was fairly sure I had. But still. I'd only just woken up.

"I think I'll take a cat nap until then. Wake me up later?" I asked as nicely as I could muster.

"Very well, sweet dreams," Voice said as my couch slid away from the wall and flattened. A butter-yellow crocheted blanket poured from the wall as I brought my legs up to the couch. I laid my head on the pillow and draped the tiny crocheted blanket over my sweet little girl, careful not to wake her or place the blanket too close to her face. It was a wonder that this blanket had survived the two boys before her. And I was so grateful because making it was way outside my wheelhouse. I was used to coding and hardware. Crocheting with my hands was how I was trying to naturally bring down my blood pressure when I was pregnant.

I remember seeing William becoming attached to it, starting to stroke it while he sucked his thumb. Carrying it from his crib to other rooms in the flat. I was already pregnant with Elijah and didn't have the time or interest in making another one, so I bought him a brand-new teddy bear, which we said was a gift from Elijah, and he loved them both instantly. Elijah slept with the blanket, too, but never seemed to attach to it. He was much more interested in his big brother and our dog, Rosie. Now that was a real sweetheart.

Once, the boys played outside my baby girl's window as she napped under that blanket. They hit her window with a rock, and the windowpane cracked. I knew they were just being kids and meant no harm, but in that moment, I made a promise to that sweet girl, my little Alli, that I would always protect her. That moment brought out a different maternal strength in me than raising my boys did. My girl slept through the whole thing—the cracked window, my lecture to the boys, their whining about being scolded, and, finally, me giving them hugs and encouraging them to play in a different part of the courtyard during nap time. New freedom for them. Sleep, peaceful sleep, for her.

"It is time to prepare for your communication session," Voice said. I stretched, rubbed my nose, and elongated that spot in my lower back that always bothers me. I looked around the room and slowly woke up. Something about this space was familiar, but I couldn't quite put my finger on it.

"What is that?" I asked.

"It's a screen for the call with your daughter, Allison," Voice responded.

"I don't have a daughter. What are you talking about? Stop testing me." My heart pounded in my chest. I knew I was too snappy, but I didn't feel like apologizing to our digital overlord.

"Your vital signs are quite elevated, Evelyn. Would you like a guided meditation to help you relax before the call?"

A light mist hissed out of the ceiling. I threw my legs over the side of the bed I was sleeping on. Suddenly, the bed started moving, and the right side rose behind me to form a couch. Clever. I stood as quickly as I could and sprinted to where I assumed the exit to this oversized coffin was hidden. It took me longer than expected, but I reached the wall. I wanted to trace along the wall with the tips of my fingers, but my balance and breath decided I should rest my whole body against it.

"Evelyn, breathe in through your nose and out through your mouth," Voice said.

"What's that?" I asked.

"It's a screen for the call," Voice replied.

———

Allison doubled her shawl sweater over her, pulling it and holding it with crossed arms. Patrick sat beside her and interacted with the screen to connect the call. Allison's breath vibrated audibly. Patrick slid his other hand to her knee.

The screen connected, and Dr. Park appeared on the screen.

"Hello, Allison and Patrick," she said without emotion.

Allison opened her mouth to speak and caught her breath.

"Hi, Dr. Park," Patrick replied.

"Please be advised that Evelyn shows continued agitation, disorientation, and disconnect. The analysis of her waking state shows further signs of terminal deterioration," Dr. Park started.

"The dream report from earlier—we got it. It was accurate. It was memory-based. I know that story!" Allison said, her sweater falling open.

"Disassociating with this reality often includes revisiting past experiences with the inability to maintain those memories in the waking state," Dr. Park said as though she had said it many times before on this very day. "Based on her current vital signs, her termination is predicted to be tomorrow."

"What?!" Patrick said. "You said this phase lasts two weeks."

"It can take that long... Evelyn appears to be progressing more quickly."

"Have we tried everything?" Allison asked softly.

"None of the therapies or triggers we've introduced in the past one hundred and four days have elicited a waking-state recognition of her living family citizens. And the termination process is already underway as per our last communication and the agreement."

Allison looked at Patrick and then down at her hands. She ran her finger across a callus under her ring finger. "Okay," she said without looking up. "Let's connect."

———

The screen changed from the bubbling brook to two people facing the camera. They looked like they were in a home. Cozy. I remember something like that once, but it was somewhere different. The woman looked like she was holding back tears, but also held a glimmer of horror in her face. Strange. What could an old lady like me do to her when I'm here in this place? I sighed and looked around my room, but remembered that there was no one here to acknowledge my annoyance except that stupid voice. It would understand, but probably wouldn't have the sense to rescue me from this. God, I missed humans.

"Hi, Evelyn," the man said. "How are you today?"

That name again. I've gotten used to everyone calling me names that aren't mine, but sometimes I feel like I should know other people's names when I talk to them. Or at least I should ask.

"You're not one of my doctors," I said more curtly than I intended.

"No, we are your family," the woman spat at the screen.

"You don't look like my Elijah," I said to the man, leaning

closer to get a better look. "My boy has darker hair. And he's more handsome, too." I inhaled through my nose and looked around the room for anything to rescue me. A lamp. The couch. A door. The door. The bathroom! I tried to stand, but the couch seemed lower than standard. A walker came out of the wall and over to me.

"Mom, I love you. You were a great mom and an amazing person."

Standing, finally, I turned back to the screen. "Were?" And I suddenly had the strength to push myself completely out of this conversation. Then I paused. The screen had rotated as I moved across the room. I turned back and used the walker to face it and get a little closer.

"Listen, honey, I don't know who your mom is. Someone's got their wires crossed. You seem... kind... so I'm sure your mom was great to you. As for me, I've gotta go to the ladies'. I'll tell them they messed up the connection, and I do hope you find her. Take care, now."

I turned my walker toward the bathroom door, which opened when I got close.

"Turn it off," I whispered, hoping Voice would hear me. Luckily, it did. The pathetic whimpering sound finally stopped, and the screen slid back into the wall. I turned to go back to the couch.

The lights around the edges of the ceiling turned indigo, and a curtain of mist slowly closed over me. I settled into the couch.

"It's time to rest," Voice said, and I agreed. This place was starting to get on my nerves. I lay on the couch, and a quilt poured over me. The quilt was made of an odd collection of fabrics. Old T-shirt graphics, small pieces of cotton. I touched one that looked like peach fleece.

One spring, we had a very late winter storm, and I ran out to buy snow gear for the kids. We didn't get snow very much where we lived then, and so we never had three little perfectly sized snow outfits. My littlest was tall for her age but refused to wear any of her brothers' hand-me-downs because she loved the colors of spring, and they wanted everything in blues and blacks. I found one of her brothers' old jackets that would fit her perfectly and bleached it, knowing that the way color theory and fabric production worked then meant there was an undertone of green, yellow, or red.

The jacket turned peach as a mother-of-pearl. She loved it so much she wore it until the sleeves nearly reached her elbows. And I have to say, the color suited her.

REVIEWS

Thank you for reading Evidence of the Future, Vol. 1! Reviews from readers like you help more people discover these stories.

Please leave a review here.

Your feedback helps me continue writing stories like this.

-Elizabeth

ABOUT THE AUTHOR

Elizabeth Eadie is an author exploring the intersection of technology and humanity. She lives in Alexandria, Virginia, where she writes speculative fiction that examines how emerging technologies reshape our relationships, our work, and our understanding of what it means to be human.

Evidence of the Future, Vol. 1 is her debut collection.

Connect with Elizabeth at elizabetheadie.com.

Vol. 2 is coming soon!